F

CLAIRE KENT

This book is a work of fiction. Names, characters, places, and incidents are the product of the author's imagination or are used fictitiously. Any resemblance to actual events, locales, or persons, living or dead, is coincidental.

Copyright © 2016 by Claire Kent. All rights reserved, including the right to reproduce, distribute, or transmit in any form or by any means.

ONE

A wolf chased Lenna into a tree. The irony would have been hilarious had she not been running for her life.

She'd lived most of her life on spacecraft, and the remainder had been spent on civilized planets where she could find good food, decent drink, and worthwhile entertainment. A couple of years ago, she'd gone on a lunar safari, but only because the guy she'd been sleeping with at the time had insisted. Otherwise, the only wild she liked in her life was flying under Coalition radar in her smuggling missions.

She'd certainly never expected to startle a sabretooth wolf and be forced to flee through the tangled undergrowth of an alien forest to get away from it.

She didn't actually know what kind of animal was chasing her. But it was shaped like a wolf—with slightly longer ears and with enormous, curled fangs like the sabretooth cats from Earth's prehistory.

Whatever the animal was, she'd clumsily stumbled across its path a minute ago. Unlike the other large mammals she'd encountered in the forest, this one didn't let her slip away undisturbed.

With a menacing growl, the wolf had lunged at her, snapping. So Lenna had done what any reasonable person would have done in such a situation.

She'd run away as fast as she could.

She was in decent shape from years of making quick escapes in her less-than-legal activities, but she didn't have a chance of outrunning the wolf. After fewer than twenty steps, it closed in on her—so quickly she could feel it snarling and panting at the back of her legs.

In desperation, she grabbed a low branch with both of her hands and swung herself up into the tree like a gymnast.

That had been the plan, anyway.

She was neither as strong nor as coordinated as a gymnast, but she did manage to get her upper body above the branch and haul her legs up, just as the wolf lunged for them. The effort felt like it would rip her biceps in two, and the forward momentum almost forced her into a face-first fall over the other side of the heavy branch.

She didn't have time to orient herself. The wolf took another leap for her, catching a piece of her pants in its mouth and grazing her shin with one of its fangs. Almost choking in panic, Lenna lurched sideways toward the tree trunk as she groped for more stability. She reached for a higher branch, scrabbling up in such a frantic climb that she scraped the skin of her hands and shredded the other leg of her pants.

She managed to pull herself higher up the tree, just out of range of the wolf's jaws.

It was ridiculous. Lenna—twenty-nine-year-old pilot and smuggler—treed by an enraged sabretooth wolf.

Oh, how far she'd fallen.

After a planet dump, however, anything could happen.

Lenna had been wandering through this miserable forest for more than two days, ever since a criminal enforcement unit had dropped her alone on this planet in an disposal pod—in what was quickly becoming the Coalition's most common form of criminal punishment. The death sentence was forbidden—mostly for PR reasons—so criminals were sentenced to a planet dump like her or a lifetime on a prison planet.

Either one usually ended up being a death sentence anyway. The Coalition could just pretend they hadn't actually pulled the trigger.

In some ways, she knew she was more fortunate than other victims of planet dumps. At least this planet was genuinely habitable to humans. The climate here was temperate, and the vegetation—even in this damned, endless forest—wasn't as foreign as she'd been expecting.

So far the only violent predator she'd encountered was the wolf who was still snarling at her feet.

But that didn't mean her punishment was an easy one.

Only a few criminals had ever made it back from planet dumps. Being dropped on an unknown planet in an unknown solar system with no provisions, weapons, or transportation—with only a disposal pod manufactured to be cheap, biodegradable, and impossible to hotwire for flight—didn't allow for many survivors.

Lenna still didn't know how long she could survive.

All she'd eaten since she'd gotten here were some root vegetables she'd scavenged. They were sort of like turnips, and they tasted like shit. She'd seen some docile animals that looked like small bears eating them so she'd figured they wouldn't kill her. She had some trouble forcing them down raw, but at least they might keep her alive.

Her pod had landed not far from a fresh-water stream, and she'd been following it south when she'd run into the wolf. She was hoping to discover new plants as she traveled and maybe something tastier to eat.

At the moment, however, eating was the least of her worries. The wolf had stopped lunging up at her, but it was still stalking around the base of the tree.

Feeling nervous and insecure, she pulled herself up to a higher branch, stabilizing herself with her back to the trunk and with both of her hands on nearby branches.

She then noticed a snake coiled up a couple of branches away—it was brownish, with subtle diamond-shaped shadings running down its back.

Lenna jerked instinctively as she saw it. The snake was just sleeping, however, so she talked herself out of her concern.

Snakes were easy. On Earth, they didn't attack unless you threatened them, and they seemed to have the same personalities here. But that didn't mean Lenna wasn't paralyzed as she darted her eyes between the coiled reptile and the pacing wolf. She almost felt like laughing, in bitter irony rather than humor.

What the hell was she *doing* here?

A noise beneath the tree distracted her, and she saw a small mammal—it looked like a large rodent of some kind—darting into the clearing at the base of the tree. When it saw the wolf, it turned quickly and sprinted away. But the wolf had seen it, and—evidently preferring easier prey—took off after the new arrival.

Lenna waited several minutes before she was brave enough to climb down again.

The whole thing was surreal. She wasn't a survivalist. She'd been in dangerous situations before, but they'd always been threats from other people and not from wildlife.

And she'd always had a gun and a ship to get her out of trouble.

Yet here she was, rooting around in an alien wilderness for food and barely escaping wild animals.

Lenna had always considered herself confident and cynical. She'd been orphaned at fifteen and living on her own ever since. She was more than capable of making her way through a complex, sophisticated world on her own. She'd used her wits and her skills to handle boorish men, hostile customers, and a totalitarian government.

This wasn't the world she knew, however, and she was realistic enough to admit that she wasn't going to make it here for long.

Shaking herself off, she reoriented her sense of direction and then retraced her steps. All she could do was find the stream again and keep walking, since she couldn't risk losing her one source of water. Her feet were aching, and the cuts on her hands and shins were stinging, even after she'd washed them as best she could. Every muscle in her body was hurting, particularly the biceps she'd pulled so brutally in her attempt to haul herself up into the tree.

Lenna was as miserable as she'd ever been, but she forced herself to keep moving forward.

If she didn't, she would die for sure.

It was late on the third day—she didn't have a timekeeper, but she suspected that the days here were longer than twenty-four hours—when she noticed the vegetation was starting to change.

Feeling a new hope, she summoned the remains of her energy and sped up her trudging. The foliage above her was finally starting to clear, and she saw some plants that looked like they needed more sunlight than could be found in the depths of the woods.

Maybe she was finally going to clear the forest.

She was so intent on getting out of the trees that she almost missed something very promising just at her feet. She might not have noticed it at all had she not stubbed her toe on a tree root.

Swearing under her breath, she stopped and looked down at her aching foot, noticing that her shoes were getting worn.

That was when she saw the green leaves—green leaves that looked a lot like leaves she knew from Earth. Panting, she crouched down and pushed aside the leaves to discover little red berries. They looked a lot like raspberries, and the broad leaves would have hidden the berries completely had she not been intentionally looking for them.

She picked one and nibbled it carefully.

It was sweet and berry-ish. So she picked some more, stuffing them into her mouth ravenously.

If they were poisonous, she'd be in big trouble. But at this point she couldn't make herself care.

When she'd eaten all of the berries in sight, she got up again and kept walking, keeping her eyes near the ground.

Several minutes later, she found some more berries.

She picked all of those too, but this time she collected them in the loose pockets of her trousers.

She didn't know how widespread the berries would be, and it would be a shame to eat them all at once if there weren't going to be anymore.

Keeping the berries safe, she kept walking as fast as she could. It was starting to get darker, and she didn't want to spend another terrified night alone in this forest.

Maybe, if she could ever break out of it, she could find civilization. And, if she found civilization, maybe she could find a way off this horrible planet. At this point, it was her only hope.

A bird fluttered to her right, making her choke out a startled sound. But, when she saw it wasn't dangerous, she leaned down and picked up a rock—trying to aim well enough to knock it unconscious.

The rock she'd thrown barely grazed the bird, and it flew away before she could try again.

She'd tried to kill a small mammal yesterday with similar lack of success. She wasn't a hunter. The closest she'd come to killing animals was swatting at bugs.

It was pretty dumb to think she could kill an animal with her bare hands and eat it.

She wasn't even sure she could make a fire.

With a sigh, she started munching on a few more of her berries—feeling better, even with the small sustenance they provided.

Less than an hour later, she finally cleared the forest and saw a huge grassy plain stretched out before her.

It was almost dark now, and it would be crazy to explore any further when she was dead tired and couldn't see anything. So she looked around on the edge of the forest until she found a large rock that provided some shelter.

Then she curled up as comfortably as she could—it wasn't very comfortable—and tried to rest.

It got cool at night, but not cold enough to require a blanket. And so far, none of the wild animals had troubled her. But it was nearly impossible to sleep well when you were starving, exhausted, and on edge, so she dozed as much as she could and waited until morning.

After several hours, she must have fallen asleep after all. Because, when she woke up, it was daylight.

Something felt immediately weird, even before she opened her eyes. She couldn't really figure out why, other than the fact that she hadn't expected to fall asleep. She was disoriented, and every muscle in her body hurt. Plus, there was a painful vacancy in her stomach from the lack of food.

But all of that was to be expected. She'd been stranded on a primitive planet with no possessions except the clothes on her back.

What she *didn't* expect, and what immediately put her on alert, was the feeling that something—or someone—was hovering above her.

The sensation made her skin prickle on her neck and her forearms.

So, instead of opening her eyes all the way, she peeked out through her slitted eyelids.

She was on her side with her back to the big rock, and the first thing she saw was a long expanse of grass.

Since it looked normal, with nothing dangerous or unusual visible, she opened her eyes all the way. It was still early morning but already bright.

With a long inhale, she rolled over onto her back.

That was when she saw it. Or him. It was hard to tell *what* it was.

Her first thought was a blond gorilla, although the climate and environment was all wrong for that kind of primate. The creature was looming over her, big and hairy, and Lenna was so shocked that she momentarily froze in stunned paralysis.

Her mouth completely dry, she could barely take a breath. The beast was too big for a gorilla, she realized now, and it didn't really look like one anyway.

Her next thought was Big Foot, like the ancient legends they used to tell on Earth. It was standing upright like a man, but its face was in shadow. And there seemed to her glazed eyes to be thick, dark hair all over its body.

Then it made a noise—a rough kind of grunt.

Lenna was slammed with a fear so intense that she was afraid she might be sick.

It moved, stepping back slightly out of the shadow.

With the change in position, Lenna could see the features on its face more clearly, and she realized it wasn't an animal after all.

It was humanoid. Maybe even human.

Its body wasn't covered in hair as she'd originally thought. Instead, it was wearing some kind of tunic made of dirty animal skins.

At first, this recognition relieved Lenna. It wasn't a wild animal looking for an easy meal. "Hi," she croaked, forcing the words out through her parched throat.

She spoke the common tongue of Coalition space—the one language nearly everyone in the civilized world could speak. There was no reason to believe this Neanderthal would understand her, but she wanted to show it she could speak.

At the sound of her voice, the Neanderthal jerked back with another grunt. Then its features transformed with an emotion that was unmistakably rage, even on such an animalistic face.

It raised the long spear she hadn't even noticed it was carrying.

Lenna was still lying on her back on the ground, completely helpless, completely disoriented.

She was a normal woman—a pilot and a mercenary but mostly civilized. She should not be here, lost and starving on the edge of a primitive forest, about to be killed by an angry Neanderthal.

Her vision tunneled into precise focus, staring at the raised spear.

Then, as the Neanderthal made a sound like a roar, her instincts suddenly kicked in. Lenna pushed her body into a clumsy roll, just as the spear descended toward her chest.

The spear connected with force, driving into the dirt she'd just been lying on. Her blood pounding in her veins, Lenna tried to focus enough to scramble to her feet.

Before she could stand up, however, the creature pulled up its spear and thrust it at her again. She rolled once again, desperation guiding her movements more than strategy.

She avoided the sharp point—which looked to be made out of some sort of stone—but it snagged the side of her shirt, pinning her to the ground.

She pulled on her shirt as hard as she could, hearing the fabric rip as she did so.

It was tearing, but not fast enough

The Neanderthal was snarling now, and it raised a fist to strike her.

Lenna tried to prepare for the blow, her mind whirling with both panic and survival instincts.

But before she felt the blow, something streaked out of the air and slammed into the Neanderthal's back.

The creature froze momentarily with the same violent grimace on its hairy face. Then it fell forward, landing just beside Lenna with a spear in its back, one that looked a lot like the one the Neanderthal had been using.

She whimpered as she tried to pull herself away, but she was still trapped by her damned shirt.

Something had killed the Neanderthal before it could kill her, and she didn't know whether to be relieved or even more terrified.

Whoever or whatever had thrown the spear was approaching. Lenna could hear it moving through the grass.

Then it too was looming over her.

This one looked more human, although, like the Neanderthal, it had such long hair and thick beard that his face was barely distinguishable. The dark eyes looked more conscious, more intelligent.

Of course, that could be Lenna's imagination or a trick of the light, but it was reassuring nonetheless.

Getting tired of lying at the feet of various cavemen, Lenna yanked as hard as she could on her shirt.

It ripped, leaving a gaping tear from the hem to her right armpit, but at least she was free from the Neanderthal's spear.

She stumbled to her feet and stared at the hairy man. He, like the Neanderthal, was dressed in an animal skin tunic, although his was less coarse and looked better crafted. He was taller than the Neanderthal, but he was just as dirty, sweaty, and primitive.

Plus, he didn't smell very good.

Lenna held her torn shirt in place and demanded, "Who are you?"

He turned to look at her, as if he'd just noticed she was there. Then what she could see of his forehead wrinkled and he took a step closer to her.

Lenna tensed, preparing to flee. But he didn't have a weapon in his hands, and when he reached out it wasn't in violence.

He held her by shoulder and peered at her, obviously as curious about her as she was about him.

Feeling strangely reassured by his inquisitive inspection, Lenna didn't resist.

She knew enough about hostile encounters to know that acting like there was something to fear sometimes *created* something to fear.

The Hairy Man had very nice eyes, she couldn't help but notice—so dark they almost looked black, large, and almost velvety.

But the rest of him was so unkempt it was hard to tell if he was sapient or not.

He leaned forward as he studied her face. Then he took some of her hair in his big, dirty hand and peered at it. Her hair was blond, and it seemed to confuse him. It couldn't have been the color, since the Neanderthal had been blond as well, so maybe it was just that her hair was mostly clean and untangled. He was snuffling a lot, and he'd occasionally grunt out a monosyllable.

Then he looked lower, down to her body. Lenna didn't stop him until he brought a hand down to her shirt, as if he were going to pull the fabric away and expose her breasts.

There were limits to the extent she'd accept a courtesy inspection by some sort of grunting, snuffling caveman.

He looked briefly annoyed when she swatted his hand away, but then he appeared to lose interest in her completely.

He'd turned back to the dead Neanderthal when Lenna glanced out to the grassy plain and noticed more humanoids approaching. Some were too far away to see clearly, but the two closest ones looked a lot like the Hairy Man—one's hair was graying, and the other was shorter and even more revolting.

When those two arrived, they all began to grunt at each other, and Lenna realized that they weren't wordless Neanderthals after all.

They seemed to be speaking a real language. It wasn't one she could understand, of course, but they appeared to be using organized speech and not just grunting and gesticulating as a pre-lingual species would do.

As she was concentrating on the guttural, incoherent conversation, another man approached without her noticing.

When she heard a fourth voice from behind her, she almost jumped. She whirled around to look at the newcomer and jerked in surprise.

It was one of the most beautiful men she'd ever seen in her life.

Unlike the other ones, this one wasn't covered in hair. He was clean-shaven, and his long dark hair was restrained in a sleek braid that fell down his back. His skin was smooth and tanned, and the muscles of his arms and legs—which weren't covered by the animal skin tunic he wore—rippled gorgeously.

The two other men who followed were also well-groomed, although not as attractive as the first one. Lenna couldn't tell if she was dealing with two different species of humanoid here, or if half of them cared about hygiene and half didn't.

The Gorgeous One gave her a dismissive glance and turned to say something to the Hairy Man.

The Hairy Man responded, gesturing toward the slain Neanderthal.

Lenna couldn't understand anything the men were saying, although she listened carefully, trying to detect any familiar words. They looked so much like humans that she couldn't believe they were a true alien species—at least, not completely. But, if they were human or part-human, they would have had to get to this planet somehow, long enough ago for any memory of civilization to have vanished.

Lenna couldn't recognize any words at all, so she had no evidence of their ancestors originally speaking an Earth language. But she was able to discern that they were discussing the death of the first man. The Gorgeous One even stepped over and spit on the body.

It wasn't a hard gesture to interpret—on any planet.

Lenna was starting to wonder if she'd been rescued at all. No one seemed to care that she was unharmed. Maybe the Hairy Man had killed the first man just to kill him. Not to save her life.

She was glad to be alive—whatever the motivation for her rescue—but she would prefer for someone to acknowledge her presence. After all, she was hoping these strangers might be of some help to her.

She was so distracted by the conversation that she didn't notice the short, revolting one had approached her from behind, until she felt his hands on her shirt. He pulled away the torn fabric to reveal her skin, making a noise that was recognizably one of sleazy interest.

Lenna gasped in surprise and reacted instinctively. She turned on her heel and kicked out her right leg, hitting him squarely in the groin with her foot. At least, it *should* be his groin, if he was made like a human male.

Apparently, he was. He huffed out in pain and bent over, just as any man on any planet in Coalition space would have done.

Lenna was used to taking care of herself, and she wasn't about to put up with any victimization, even if she was abandoned and alone on this freakish, primitive world.

But, after she'd lashed out, she realized how vulnerable her position was. She had no protection here, and she'd just struck one of the six males surrounding her. The others might not appreciate it. After all, by all appearances, these hunter-gatherer types had rather old-fashioned sensibilities.

But the others didn't defend their comrade. They looked over curiously, and the Gorgeous One sneered at the man she'd kicked, muttering something snide.

The Hairy Man made a series of snorts and huffs. It wasn't until she looked in his dark eyes that she realized he was actually laughing.

Evidently, seeing his revolting companion hit by a female amused him.

Lenna looked back suspiciously at the one she'd kicked, who was still bent over and moaning. She figured he'd be mad about being so humiliated, and she had no idea how he'd react.

She tensed when he straightened up and snarled at her, taking two steps over with obvious aggression.

But the Hairy Man barked out a sharp word that brought the other to a sudden stop.

Lenna looked back curiously, trying to figure out if the Hairy Man was trying to protect her or if he just despised the other man. Since the Hairy Man was glaring coldly at the other one, she leaned toward the latter interpretation.

Even now, none of them appeared particularly concerned about her, but at least they hadn't decided to let that disgusting half-animal have his way with her.

The others were still talking, completely disregarding her existence. During the discussion, the Hairy Man went over and retrieved his spear from the first man's back.

Still talking, all six of them turned around and started to walk away.

Lenna blinked. "What the hell?" she muttered.

Were they actually going to leave her here?

"Hey!" she called out, running after them. "Hey! Wait! Wait!"

They turned around, and the Gorgeous One's mouth curled up in annoyance. He said something to her, but she couldn't understand what it was.

"Can I come with you?" She ran over to him, looking up at him pleadingly, searching for some way to make her request clear.

They didn't seem to be the most generous of people, but at least they might be able to protect her from wild animals and give her something to eat. She wasn't a fool. She'd stand a much better chance of surviving with them than she would by herself.

The Gorgeous One—who she was now suspecting was the leader—gave her a cursory once-over and sneered again.

Lenna had always known herself to be an attractive woman, and she'd had plenty of male attention over the years. But evidently nothing about her face or body was appealing to the man in front of her.

Since he wasn't going to be swayed by attraction or kindness, she racked her mind for something she could offer him. All she had in her possession were the berries she'd found earlier. So, just before he turned away from her again, she stuck her hand in her pocket and thrust the half-crushed berries out at him.

He jerked back in surprise and peered at the red berries with narrowed green eyes.

The Hairy Man grunted out some sort of question, which the leader answered dismissively. Then the leader turned away from her again.

Lenna, realizing she was losing her last chance at protection, noticed the Hairy Man was still looking at her curiously.

So she ran over to him and offered the berries. She felt like an absolute idiot—trying to give smashed berries to a dirty caveman—but she was too frantic to care.

The Hairy Man carefully picked one of the berries out of her hand. Then he lifted it higher to study it, the upper part of his face—the only part that wasn't covered with hair—conveying obvious confusion.

Realizing that he didn't even know what the berry was for, Lenna took one of them and put it in her mouth, with exaggerated slowness. "Mmm," she murmured.

The Hairy Man frowned and raised the berry to his mouth. As soon as he tasted it, his expression changed. He grunted something, and then looked at her, as if she were supposed to understand what he said.

Lenna shrugged and offered him the rest of her handful of berries.

He took them, eating a couple more.

Nodding, he called out something to the others, who had already started walking away.

The leader stopped and looked back at the Hairy Man. After some more discussion, he finally came over and ate one of the berries himself.

After even more talk, he went over and took something off the belt of one of the other groomed men. Then he brought it over to Lenna.

It was an empty leather sack. The handsome leader handed it to Lenna with a few words she didn't understand.

He turned away and started walking again.

Lenna stared at the sack in bewilderment. Instinctively, she looked up at the Hairy Man, who was still standing beside her.

Evidently reading her questioning expression, the man took the last berry in his hand and dropped it into the sack. Then he made another gesture, clearly telling her that she was to follow them.

He too started to walk away.

But now Lenna understood. She was allowed to go with them. And, in return, she had to fill up this sack with berries.

She would have preferred to be a welcomed guest, but this was better than nothing.

At least she'd have some chance of survival.

So she jogged after them, hoping that she'd find enough berries, now that she'd cleared the forest. The ones she'd found before were all in the forest. There were clusters of trees around, though, even in the grassy plain, so she still had some hope.

They walked for over an hour, and Lenna had to work to keep up. Now that they'd started, they didn't even acknowledge her existence, except for the Hairy Man, who glanced back at her occasionally and made impatient gestures for her to hurry up.

Under normal circumstances, Lenna walked just fine. But she'd been on her feet for almost three days, and she had cuts and bruises all over her body. Plus, she kept having to stop whenever she recognized the leaves that hid the berries she was supposed to collect.

Frankly, it was very annoying to be constantly rushed under these circumstances.

The large cut on her shin from the wolf's fang was burning so intensely now she had trouble focusing on anything else. So, when she saw another patch of berries beneath a tree, she didn't kneel down or crouch, but rather sat down completely in the hope of relieving some of the strain on her skin.

She started picking the berries, relieved to see how many there were here. In a few minutes, her sack was almost three-fourths of the way full.

She was about to get up when she felt strong arms on her sides, hauling her up from behind.

With a startled shriek, she kicked her legs out and jerked her head back to see who it was.

The Hairy Man. His big hands were spanning her ribs, and one of them was in direct contact with her skin, just under her breast, since her torn shirt had fallen open.

It wasn't a sexual advance, though. She realized that almost immediately. He was grunting at her again, his tone rough and bossy.

Fed up with this treatment, Lenna snapped. "Let go of me, you asshole. I'm tired and injured, and you're making me pick these damned berries!"

He'd lifted her up to her feet, but he hadn't released her yet. Her angry voice appeared to surprise him. He paused briefly before he grunted some more.

Lenna felt a little hysterical, and she had to stifle a laugh. This was absurd. They couldn't understand each other, and yet they were bickering as if they could.

She struggled in his grip, gasping when she felt one of his fingers against the underside of her breast.

He let her go, so abruptly that her knees buckled.

She fell forward, crying out at the pain in her feet and legs.

His face was really hard to read because of the ridiculous beard, but his eyes narrowed now, and he lowered himself onto the ground beside her.

They had a brief scuffle as he tried to take possession of one of her legs—the one with the throbbing cut.

He was snuffling when she finally let him look at it, and it was freaking her out. He'd leaned over, like he was smelling it.

Disgusted, Lenna looked away. If he did anything too weird, she was going to have give up on him.

But he didn't even touch the cut. Instead, he just stood up and walked away.

"Well, fine," she muttered. "Go ahead and leave me here. I've never met such an ugly, selfish, smelly, rude…"

She was still listing her grievances when the Hairy Man returned.

He was carrying some leaves, and he was muttering under his breath too. If his expression was anything to go on, he was as annoyed with her as she was with him.

"I don't know what your problem is," she said, although she knew he couldn't understand, "*I'm* the one at a disadvantage here. It wasn't like I got hurt just to slow you down."

He ignored her and crushed the leaves in his palm. Then he took hold of her ankle and stretched out her leg.

Before she realized what he was doing, he smeared the leaves onto the deep, painful cut.

She whimpered slightly as the leaves stung the wound, but, before she could object or pull away, the sensations grew blessedly numb. The leaves must be painkillers.

"Oh. Thanks." She didn't feel particularly generous, but she realized that at least he'd been trying to help.

He stood up, looming above her. Realizing his silent demand, Lenna sighed and leaned forward to grab the sack of berries at his feet.

When she glanced up, from a different angle, she noticed something new. Something that made her twitch in surprise.

She looked away quickly and stumbled to her feet. He hadn't even offered her a hand.

He grunted something else and motioned for her to get moving, his expression impatient and annoyed.

Lenna blinked and started walking, her leg feeling a lot better, although her feet were still killing her.

Well, one of her questions was answered. This Hairy Man was definitely human—as human as the sleek, handsome leader.

At least, what she'd seen under his animal skin tunic was decidedly human. And male.

He hadn't been wearing any undergarments.

And he had been hard.

She wasn't quite sure what to do with that information, except for cringe a little bit at the thought. Hopefully, she hadn't been the thing that had turned him on. The idea of having sex with such a rough, hairy creature was not an appealing one.

Now, if the Gorgeous One offered—and wasn't an asshole—then maybe she'd consider it. But *this* one—this one couldn't even be bothered to bathe.

Surely he hadn't gotten turned on looking at her bruised, bloody leg. Things were weird enough here as it was.

He certainly wasn't acting on lust. He was already a distance ahead of her, and there had been no warmth or interest on his face.

She was stuck on this planet. That much was inevitable. And she had little chance of surviving on her own. Lenna had always been practical. It was how she'd managed to remain so completely independent all her life. She'd learned to make do with whatever help she was offered, but only for as long as she needed it.

But if a big, smelly caveman expected to have sex with her, she would have to make other plans.

For now, she wasn't going to worry about it. It could have just been a fluke. None of the men here seemed to have been swept away by her femininity.

Hurrying to keep up and trying to ignore her aching hunger and the pain in her muscles, Lenna followed the Hairy Man to wherever he was going.

Maybe it was hunting that turned him on.

TWO

The following afternoon, the Hairy Man killed a large grazing animal that moved in herds and looked a lot like a deer.

They'd been walking endlessly—and to no purpose as far as Lenna could determine—when they finally saw a small group of the animals in the distance. All of the men went after the deer, but the Hairy Man was the only one who killed one.

To Lenna's relief, this was evidently the goal of their expedition, and they immediately strung up the dead animal and turned toward some mountains in the distance to the east, carrying the carcass with them.

Lenna was weak and exhausted and anxious, but she was deeply relieved when they finally reached a large cave set in a small grouping of hills as the sun was going down. A couple dozen men, women, and children came running out of the cave to greet the hunting party.

This must be where the tribe, clan, or troupe had a permanent residence.

She had no idea what would be waiting for her here, but at least she wouldn't have to keep walking.

A few kids came up to check her out—poke her shoulder and touch her hair—but everyone else simply ignored her. It was a strange and disconcerting feeling, to be so completely irrelevant that no one even noticed her presence.

She stayed at a distance and watched, finding a mostly flat rock to sit on, catch her breath, and observe as the men started a large bonfire in the open space outside the cave and the women began to skin and gut the deer.

Everyone appeared pleased and celebratory, so large animals like this must be some kind of victory.

They cut the meat into small pieces and made a stew with about a third of it, using those turnip-like roots she'd found before and some other roots and herbs. The stew smelled delicious, and Lenna was starving. She could understand why everyone seemed so happy about the hunting party's success.

She was surprised when the Gorgeous One glanced over in her direction and then started walking toward her. She opened her mouth to say something instinctively, hoping that being acknowledged in this way was a good sign.

But her words broke off in a huff when he grabbed her by the shoulder, lifted her to her feet, and then leaned over to pick up the rock she'd been sitting on. She stared in astonishment as he carried the rock near the fire and positioned it for a pretty brunette to sit on.

He'd just taken her rock, moving her out of the way like she was an object.

"Asshole," she said, not quite quietly enough. Several people turned to look at her, as if they hadn't realized she was able to speak.

The Hairy One heard her, she noticed. He was stoking the fire, but he glanced over his shoulder at her and gave a few more of those huffs that were evidently his laughter.

Evidently, they were all assholes.

She was glaring around, wondering if this was really a group she wanted to hook up with, when she noticed the eyes of a younger man were resting on her.

She knew he was younger because his shoulders weren't as broad and his beard and hair weren't as long as the older men. He was attractive in an understated way, even though he wasn't groomed.

They shared a look that was almost understanding, and she held her breath as he moved over toward her.

She felt a surge of overwhelming relief when he reached her and asked, "Planet dump?"

She nodded, suddenly grounded in a way she hadn't since she'd gotten out of the Coalition pod. Just the fact that he spoke the common language, when no one else here did, made her feel like she wasn't completely alone. "A few days ago."

"They dumped me here three years ago," he said, keeping his eyes focused mostly on the bonfire but occasionally darting over toward her face, as if he didn't want to draw attention to their conversation.

Lenna tried to imagine being on this planet for that long. She couldn't. She just couldn't. "I'm Lenna," she said, keeping her voice low like his had been.

"Desh."

"Is there anyone else here who has been planet dumped?"

"Not in this tribe. Maybe in some of the others."

"So how did these people get here?"

"I don't know, but they've been here for generations. They speak their own language and have absolutely no idea about the rest of the universe. They're human, so they're not native to this planet, but they must have been here for a really long time."

She sighed, eyeing the tribe members as they gathered around the fire. "So I guess that means there's no way off this planet?"

Desh shook his head. "There's no technology of any kind on this planet beyond wheels and spears and hammers."

Lenna smothered a groan. "You said there are other tribes on this planet?"

"Yes. This tribe calls themselves the Kroo. It sounds like the man who attacked you—the one that Rone killed—was from the Hosh tribe, who the Kroo absolutely despise. You're better off with this tribe for sure."

"What do you mean?"

"Women are treated better with the Kroo." He met her eyes briefly. "I wouldn't leave, if I were you."

She swallowed, able to imagine all too well what might happen to her elsewhere, based solely on that first Neanderthal she'd encountered. "Understood."

She watched as the stronger, more mature males started to dish out the stew. "I'm starving."

"You won't get any stew."

"What do you mean? There's plenty of it for everyone."

"Yes, but those of us on the fringes don't get it. It's given out by the alphas, and so only those connected to them will get it."

"That's ridiculous. What about the rest of us?"

Desh stood up and walked to the far side of the bonfire, leaning over to grab a loaf of what looked like bread and some of those disgusting turnip-like roots. He brought them over to where she was still sitting on the ground.

"You're not a weakling," she said, accepting the food he offered rather begrudgingly. She was willing to eat anything at this point, and at least the bread stuff was better than the turnips. "Why don't you just go over and take a bowl of stew?"

"I'd have to fight them for it, and I'd have to win." His eyes were a very dark blue, and his expression almost unreadable. "I spent all my life in studying hard in school. I never even played sports. Do you really think I can take one of these men who've learned to hunt and fight from the time they could walk?"

Lenna looked at him in interest. She liked his matter-of-fact tone and his intelligence. She could see him as an academic type, but he was clearly more than that now. "How old are you?"

"Nineteen."

She gasped. She'd known he was young, but not that young. "You got planet dumped when you were sixteen? What did you do?"

"I said the wrong thing to the wrong person. The Coalition doesn't like to be talked back to. What did you do?"

"Smuggling." She was about to ask another question when the Hairy Man walked over toward where they were sitting, a bowl of stew in his hand. She fell silent, staring up at him as he barked out what sounded like a question.

Desh responded, and the two men had a brief conversation. Lenna assumed it was about her, since the Hairy Man kept looking at her.

If she'd hoped he might offer her some of the stew, she was sorely disappointed when he turned his back and walked away.

"What was that about?" she asked, staring at the man's straight back and broad shoulders in the animal skins he wore.

"He wanted to know how I knew your language."

"What did you tell him?"

"I said we come from the same place. Then he wanted to know where we come from. I just said far away." Desh gave an amused snort. "Then he asked if you come from the sky—which I think they consider like heaven."

"That's just great. He thinks I'm an angel, but he still won't give me a bowl of stew."

"Get used to it."

"What is his name anyway?"

"Rone." Desh nodded over toward the Gorgeous One. "That's Tamen. He's the lead alpha, but Rone is always nipping at his heels. Rone is a few years younger, but I've never seen anyone hunt like him. I'd bet he could be lead alpha soon, if he decides he wants it."

For some reason, this pleased Lenna. Rone hadn't been remotely nice to her, but at least he'd acknowledged her existence, something that Tamen hadn't really done.

"So why are some of the men shaved and clean but most of them not?" she asked after a moment.

"Women groom the men. The men with women get groomed. The others don't."

"Why doesn't Rone have a woman, if he's an alpha?"

"He hasn't chosen one yet." He gestured over toward where Rone was sitting, finishing off his stew. "Watch."

Lenna watched as a young woman approached him, standing beside him and then stroking his hair. Rone kept eating, saying a few words to the woman and then finally getting up and walking away from her.

"Women make the advances," Desh explained, "but the men choose their mates. The women have some agency in this tribe, but it's still a patriarchal culture." He turned to look at her, eyeing her up and down. "You're pretty. Your best bet is probably to pick out a man and make a move on him, and he might respond and make you his mate. Pick as high as you think you can go."

Lenna glanced over at Taman, who was evidently the highest rung in the tribe's hierarchy. He really was very handsome, but he didn't even look at her like she was a person. She couldn't imagine being his "mate."

"He's groomed, though. He already has a woman, doesn't he?"

"Yes. This tribe is monogamous with their mates, but they don't necessarily mate for life. When men get bored, they move on to new mates. Tamen is on his fourth woman since I've been here."

Lenna made a face. "That doesn't sound like a good deal to me."

"But they're responsible for taking care of their previous mates, so once you're the mate of an alpha, you're set for life—at least as long as the man continues to have authority in the tribe. I'm not saying it's a great deal for you, but it's probably the best way to secure your position. Otherwise, you're stuck on the fringes with the loners and orphans."

Lenna watched Tamen for several minutes, and she felt nothing but disgust at the idea of being his woman. Maybe that was the smartest thing for her to do, but she wasn't going to do it.

Not yet, anyway.

She'd made it this far in life without subjecting herself to the whims of another person. Her independence had always been the most important thing to her. She might be in desperate straights here, but she wasn't quite that desperate yet.

The Kroo stayed around the bonfire, eating and socializing until the moon was high in the sky. Then everyone went back into the cave.

The cave was large and open, scattered with beds made of furs and grasses. It didn't take Lenna long to figure out that the beds were for the alphas and their women and families. Those on the fringes like her didn't get a bed.

She didn't even get an animal skin for a blanket.

It wasn't a cold night, though, and she was exhausted. So she found a spot that was mostly clean where she could lay with her back to the wall, giving her some sense of safety.

Desh had said that women were treated better in this tribe, but she still felt very vulnerable in a cave full of men who didn't seem to see her as a real person.

She wasn't far from Rone's bed, and he felt safer to her than the others. He might not help her, but he wouldn't hurt her. There was comfort in that.

She closed her eyes and tried to drown out the overwhelming smell of dirt and body odor, and the sound of couples having sex around the cave.

She was tired enough that she actually went to sleep.

Lenna spent most of the next day picking more berries. None of the women had said a word to her—they acted like she wasn't even present. But Lenna was hanging around aimlessly after the morning meal, wondering what she should do, when Rone came over to her and handed her the sack she'd used to collect the berries on the previous day.

He didn't say anything, and she wouldn't have been able to understand him if he did, but the meaning was very clear.

She was supposed to gather more berries. That was evidently her task in this tribe, in return for which they would feed her (at least a little) and keep her safe from predators.

It was a better deal than getting eaten by sabretooth wolves, so she started searching the growth beneath the copses of trees near the cave. They were far from the deep woods now, and the landscape was hilly, with a lot of large rocks and wide stretches of grassland. But there were groupings of trees scattered around, so that was where she went to look for berries.

The tribe had spread out to a variety of tasks—some staying near the cave and working on mending clay pots, stone tools, and clothing. Others going farther out to spear fish in the nearby river or hunt for small animals.

Lenna wasn't comfortable venturing too far out, since there were evidently hostile tribes and predatory animals around. She made sure to stay in sight of the men at the river and was pleased there were enough berries around to fill her sack.

The tribe evidently didn't eat a midday meal. When she returned to the cave with her berries, Tamen came over to take them from her hands, peering into the bag suspiciously.

Evidently, he was satisfied with her haul because he nodded and then gestured over to a pile of fresh fish, where a boy who looked around ten years old was working. Lenna watched for a moment, realizing the boy was gutting and deboning the fish.

She looked back at Tamen, who gestured her over.

Evidently, she now got the enviable task of gutting and deboning fish with a boy.

She didn't try to argue, however. She just went over, sat down, and watched him until she could figure out how to do it.

She was smart and competent. If she had to gut fish to earn her keep, then she would do so without complaining.

By evening, she was exhausted, and her fingers were raw from working on the fish. She'd cut herself numerous times on the fine, sharp bones.

The smell of meat cooking was delicious, but she was so ravenous that she didn't even complain when Desh brought her over bread and the turnip-things again. Most of the tribe sat in a large circle around the fire—she counted thirty-six of them. But she and Desh sat just behind the circle, as did a few others on the fringes. A very old woman whose mate must have died, since she no longer had a man to vouch for her. Two orphaned children. And another young man around Desh's age.

"Do the fringes ever move into the circle?" she asked Desh, after taking a bite of her bread.

"Yes. Jono, over there, was back here with me for the first year. But then he killed a boar and took a mate. He's in the circle now."

"Why was he on the outskirts before?"

"He was new to the tribe. Had no ties and hadn't proved himself as a man yet."

"Why was he new?"

"Most boys leave the tribes they were raised in when they hit puberty."

Lenna thought about this and then realized the obvious reason for it. "Ah. So that's how they avoid inbreeding."

"Yes. The boys leave and join other tribes. The women hold the tribe together, maintaining its history, character, and behavior."

"How many tribes are there on this planet?"

"I don't know. Dozens. Maybe hundreds. Since I've been here, we've encountered at least thirty others, and we've never ventured very far from this region. There could be a city on the other side of the planet, and I wouldn't know."

"You never wanted to find out?"

"I don't think there's a city. Rone came from very far away, if I'm understanding the stories about him correctly. And he knows of nothing but other tribes like this one."

Lenna turned to look at Rone—her Hairy Man—and saw that he was watching her.

He seemed to watch her a lot, but she couldn't read his expression enough to figure out why.

After a few minutes, she started to get self-conscious and turned back to Desh.

"So women always stay in the tribe they were born into?"

"Usually—unless they're kidnapped by other tribes."

"What?"

"Occasionally, another tribe will kidnap a young woman. It seems to be fairly standard practice. If there aren't enough girls born into a tribe, they need some way of getting more."

"That's terrible! Surely tribes would fight each other over that."

Desh gave a half-shrug. "Not as much as you'd think. They seem to have an understanding among themselves to avoid all-out war. Survival is the chief priority, so war has to be avoided at all costs. The only real act of war would be entering another tribe's territory. The boundaries are clearly understood, and no one has crossed those lines in the years I've been here."

"Then how are the women kidnapped?"

"In no-man's land. Tribes have to occasionally leave their territory—to hunt or scavenge food or such things. Last year, two of the Kroo girls were gathering herbs, and they were taken by the Hosh, our nearest neighbors. Tamen and the other hunters caught up with one of the girls before they reached Hosh territory, so they got her back. The other they didn't catch up to in time, so they had to let her go."

"They just let her go?" Lenna shouldn't have been surprised but she was. The families in this tribe didn'express affection the way she was used to, but they seemed to at least have a sense of loyalty.

"What choice did they have? Entering Hosh territory is an act of war, and a woman just isn't worth that."

"Nice," Lenna muttered.

"Hey, it's not my worldview. It's theirs. Anyway, a man wouldn't be worth it either. If a man is attacked or killed by another tribe, then you can seek revenge in no-man's land—but you can't cross into someone else's territory to do it. It's a different world. You're going to have to learn to adjust."

"I know." She paused, feeling depressed and so deciding to change the subject. "So you've never killed a boar?" she asked.

He shook his head. "Or any other animal. I'm not allowed in the inner circle yet. They won't even let me join the hunting parties."

"If I killed a boar, would they let me in?"

He laughed. "No. Women don't hunt. The only way you get in is if a man chooses you for a mate."

She scowled and muttered out a complaint about archaic, misogynist cultures.

Desh just laughed again. "Hey, think on the bright side. At least you can pick out a man and let him know you're interested. You're not stuck with any creep who wants you." He nodded toward Ugar, the disgusting man who'd groped her before, who was lurking unpleasantly nearby.

Lenna sneered at the revolting man and looked instinctively back toward Rone, whose dark eyes were glinting in the firelight and still focused on her.

She tried to imagine having Rone as a "mate" and couldn't even begin to wrap her mind around it. She could barely even see his face in all that hair.

The eating had mostly ended, and a couple of the men had gone to get what looked like pipes made of bone.

The music they played wasn't like any music Lenna was familiar with. It was just slow, extended noise that had the same effect of a haunting wail. One of the older women started to talk, and Lenna realized after a while that she must be telling some sort of story. The entire tribe was listening, as if spellbound.

"A tale of an ancient warrior," Desh whispered after a few minutes. "They tell this one a lot."

"What about the ancient warrior?"

"He climbed the forbidden mountain to claim fire for the tribes."

"Forbidden mountain? Is that a real thing?"

"Yes. It's in no-man's land, but you can see the peak if you look north on a clear day. Apparently no tribe ever ventures there. It's considered holy or something."

The story went on for a long time, accompanied by the sound of the music's keening notes. Lenna studied the faces around her, trying to judge from their expressions who might be nice and who she wanted to avoid.

It was difficult to tell. Only Rone and one of the women—who appeared to be a previous mate of Tamen—ever met her eyes.

Eventually, the story ended and some of the Kroo finally rose from their places. Lenna happened to be watching when a young woman went over to Rone—the same young woman who had made a move on him the previous night.

"That's Sorel," Desh said, noticing her preoccupation. "Tamen's oldest daughter. She was the one who was almost kidnapped last year but they got back. She must have decided she wanted Rone last week, because she's tried it on him for several days now."

As Lenna watched, Rone shrugged the girl away and got up, glancing over at Lenna before he walked away.

"Is he not interested in sex?"

"I'm sure he is. He just doesn't want Sorel as a mate."

"She's pretty."

"Sure. I think it has more to do with the fact that she's Tamen's daughter, and Rone doesn't want to be tied to Tamen that way."

This piece of information interested Lenna, and she thought about it as she went back to the cave with the others.

She moved to the same spot she'd slept the previous night, against the wall, close to Rone's bed. She was so caught up in her thoughts about the strange social dynamics of this tribe that she didn't notice Ugar coming up to her.

He'd grabbed her by the shoulder before she realized he was there, and she whirled around instinctively, using a self-defense move she'd learned at ten years old, flattening her hand and using the heel of it to hit Ugar in the nose.

He choked on a pained exclamation and bent over, his eyes watering from the blow.

"Stay away from me," Lenna said sharply, hoping he would understand her tone if not the words themselves.

She heard a noise from behind her and turned to see that Rone was laughing again. He'd laughed the other day when she'd fought off Ugar as well.

She wasn't sure what he found so funny about her getting groped by such a creep.

While her back was turned, Ugar reached out for her again. She was getting ready to hit him once more when Rone barked out something—loud and gruff—that evidently made Ugar stop.

Ugar muttered and glared, but he turned away and slouched back to the other side of the cave.

Lenna turned to look back at Rone, who was frowning in Ugar's direction, and she felt a wave of surprised appreciation.

She'd definitely made the right choice in sleeping near Rone. At least he didn't treat her like an object.

He stood over his bed, staring at her for a long time, almost like he was waiting for something.

She had no idea what he might be waiting for, so eventually she just gave him a little smile and lowered herself onto the ground to sleep.

THREE

For the next month, the days passed in a tedious haze of exhausting sameness.

Those on the fringes of the Kroo tribe like her and Desh were expected to work in order to keep their place. Her duties were to pick those berries, gut fish, and to clean up after meals—which was often quite a nauseating prospect since meals usually involved dead animals.

None of these duties were particularly pleasant, and they kept her busy all day. Other than talking to Desh when she could, she was alone most of the time. She always felt hungry, and she was so exhausted by the end of the days that she was asleep almost before she got into her position on the ground against the wall near Rone's bed.

One day faded into the next, and she would have lost track of time completely if she hadn't kept a running count in her head.

It was getting colder, though, and the berries were starting to die. She was beginning to get worried about how she would contribute to the tribe when there were no more berries to find.

She also hoped she wouldn't catch pneumonia trying to sleep on the floor in tattered clothes and no blanket in the middle of winter. She was still wearing the torn clothes she'd arrived in—clumsily mended the best she could. In order to have animal skins like everyone else wore, she would need to have a man to give them to her.

Early one morning, she was huddled in her position in the cave, trying not to shiver, as the tribe started to get up for the day.

She didn't want to get up. She was cold and starving and sore from how far she'd walked the day before to find the remaining berries. She looked at Rone's bed longingly, wanting to bury herself in his pile of furs.

He must have felt her watching because he glanced back toward her as he stood up. He was just as hairy and unkempt as he'd been when she'd first seen him, and only his eyes looked intelligent.

He didn't smile and didn't acknowledge her. Just scratched his arms and adjusted his clothes. He had a leather cord that he wore around his waist to keep his garment in place, but it had several tight knots in it.

He frowned at it as he tried to undo the knots with his big fingers. After a minute, he gave up and tossed the cord onto his bed, looking annoyed as if it was staying knotted on purpose just to irritate him.

In a few minutes, everyone had left the cave to eat breakfast and get started on the day.

Lenna was in no hurry to do either—since the idea of that bland bread and disgusting turnip-root just made her feel even sicker than she already did. When the cave was completely empty, she went over to Rone's bed and picked up the knotted cord.

Those knots must have been in it for months. They were so tight she couldn't even get her fingernails in between to loosen them.

What the hell had the idiot done to this thing to get it so knotted?

For no good reason, she felt a swell of determination to unknot the cord. She sat down on the ground and focused more closely, working a knot until she finally managed to loosen and then untie it. It took her more than a half-hour to get all of the knots out, but she smiled in satisfaction as she smoothed out the leather cord and laid it back on Rone's bed.

She had no idea why she'd done it. He certainly hadn't done a lot for her over the last month—except stare at her, laugh at her, and make her feel safe by his presence.

Maybe that was enough.

She was leaving the cave, knowing she needed to get busy cleaning up after breakfast or someone would get mad at her.

Rone was coming back in as she reached the cave entrance.

Desh had been teaching her the tribe's language for the last month, but she still could only understand a few words in each sentence.

It wasn't a well-developed language like the ones she was used to. It was primarily made up of nouns and verbs, with no articles, few prepositions or abstract words, and very slippery usage of direct and indirect objects.

Rone frowned and grunted something like, "Meal...late."

Evidently he was giving her a little lecture about missing breakfast when she'd been working on unknotting his damned cord.

"Sorry." She'd learned that word early on. She felt like she used it all the time—since she couldn't risk anyone in this tribe getting mad at her.

She knew for sure she would have died without them.

Rone was still glaring, but he handed her a piece of flat bread. She'd watched it being made and knew it was made out of some sort of grain, but it didn't taste nearly as good as wheat.

She blinked in surprise at the bread in his hand. He'd actually saved her some food.

When she didn't move, he thrust it at her again. "Take bread!"

She took it, staring down at it in astonishment. No one but Desh had been nice to her since she'd arrived on this planet. She didn't even know the word for "thank you."

Instead, she said, "Glad. Glad bread."

Rone was still frowning, but he gave her a nod before he walked farther into the cave.

Lenna couldn't help but pause and watch from a distance as he reached his bed. She saw him stop, staring down at what must be the cord she'd unknotted.

He picked it up slowly, stroking a finger down the leather and then raising it to his face. It looked like he was sniffing it, smelling it.

When she saw him start to look back toward her, she hurried out of the cave, eating the bread quickly before she started to work for the day.

She was glad she'd spent the time unknotting his cord.

It had been nice of him to save her the bread.

That evening, she was curling up on the floor again in her normal place, hugging her arms across her belly in an attempt to stay warm.

The cave was never quiet at night. It was one large room with a lot of people in it, so there were always the sounds of talking, of snoring, of sex.

The sex seemed to consist mostly of men taking women from behind, as far as she could tell in the dark. The men did all the grunting. It never lasted very long. Lenna wondered if the women even knew what an orgasm was.

She gasped and sat up when she was suddenly aware of a man standing above her.

Realizing it was Rone, she sighed in relief. She had no idea what he was doing, but at least he wasn't going to attack her.

She blinked a few times until she could see that he was offering her a blanket made of a soft animal skin.

Her lips parted as she stared up at him.

"Cord good," he grunted. "Blanket."

Even missing words as she did, she understood what he was saying. He was thanking her for working on unknotting his cord, and her reward was the blanket.

She accepted the blanket with a smile, wrapping it around her gratefully.

Rone was peering at her with narrowed eyes.

"Glad," she said, using the word she'd used that morning, since she'd asked Desh earlier and he'd told her there didn't seem to be a word in their language that meant thank you. "Glad blanket." She smiled at him again.

The habitual frown on his face softened. He didn't smile, but for once he didn't look grumpy. He looked vaguely astonished, as if he didn't know what was going on.

She didn't know what was going on either, but she was very happy about the blanket. It was rough and smelled like Rone, but it was warm, which was the only thing that mattered.

It still felt like Rone was watching her in the dark as she tried to go to sleep, far more comfortable than she'd been the night before.

~

The next morning, Rone gave her a bowl of stew.

It wasn't a very good stew, since it was made with the last remnants of the deer-like animal they'd killed the previous week. But since she'd had nothing but bread, berries, and turnip-roots for more than a month, she couldn't remember ever enjoying anything more.

Rone stood and watched her as she ate it, as if he suspected she wouldn't know what to do with it.

He was the strangest man she'd ever met, but at least he seemed to understand gratitude.

When she finished the bowl and he was still standing in front of her, she said, "Glad. Glad stew."

Rone nodded at her and then waited, as if he were expecting her to do something else.

She had no idea what she was supposed to do.

What the hell was he always waiting for?

After a minute, Rone scowled at her and walked away, and Lenna was left more confused than ever.

Since the meat was pretty much gone now, the alpha men left that morning to go on another hunting party. Lenna really hoped they'd kill an animal quickly so Rone would return to the cave soon. She was familiar with the Kroo now, and most of them left her alone. But a couple of the men still creeped her out, including Ugar, who was the worst of them all.

Ugar hadn't gone with the hunting party this time, so Lenna was on edge.

It was too cold now for berries, so Lenna had less work to do than she'd done before. She watched the other women, trying to figure out something else she could do to earn her keep. Most of what the women did involved taking care of their men, which wasn't any help for Lenna—who had no man.

That afternoon, she watched the women as they cleaned the animal skin blankets on their men's beds. They took them outside and then shook them off. Then they scraped them with what looked like large pine cones. Then they hung them outside on branches to air out in the sun and wind.

Remembering how grateful Rone had been when she'd unknotted his cord, Lenna decided there was no reason why she shouldn't clean his bed.

He had piles of furs on it—more than any other man but Tamen—but she lugged them all outside, taking them one by one to shake off, scrape off, and then air out in the sun.

By the state of the blankets, she wondered if they'd ever been cleaned before.

The man was really a mess. No wonder he smelled so bad.

The job took all afternoon and into the first part of the evening. It was almost dark when she was spreading the furs back out on his bed, pleased with the results of her hard work.

She wondered what Rone would do when he returned to find his nice, clean bed.

She was so busy spreading out the blankets she didn't hear anyone come up behind her.

She squealed when strong arms grabbed her and lifted her to her feet. Whirling around, she saw the man who had grabbed her was Rone. He was scowling at her and barking out something that included the words, "Rone bed."

She'd learned from Desh that their language didn't include personal pronouns, so they always referred to themselves in the third person.

"Clean," she gasped, afraid he'd thought she was claiming his bed for her own. "Lenna clean Rone bed. Clean. Clean." She gestured toward the blankets urgently.

His scowl turned into his normal suspicious frown, and he looked from her to the bed and then back again.

Then he crouched down and picked up one of the furs, sniffing it the way he had the cord.

"Clean," she said one more time.

He stared at his bed for a long time, gently stroking the blankets. Finally, he looked back up at her.

"Good?" she asked, after a long moment of just staring at each other.

Rone nodded slowly. "Good."

He stood up, standing very close to her, watching her in that way he had that morning, in that way she didn't understand.

Like he was waiting for something.

She stared back at him, suddenly hit with a wave of attraction that was beyond her comprehension.

The man was dirty, smelly, covered with hair, and totally rude. She shouldn't be attracted to him. At all. In any way.

But her body responded to his proximity, to the strength she could see in his arms, his shoulders, his chest. To the intelligence, the humanness she saw in his eyes.

For a moment, she had to fight the urge to reach out and touch him.

Then she swallowed and looked away, telling herself to get a grip. It had been a hard month for her. She probably would have responded in the same way to anyone paying her some attention.

Rone was scowling again when she looked back at him.

She had no idea why he always got so annoyed with her.

Searching for something to say that she had the vocabulary for, she finally said, "Hunt good?"

Rone nodded soberly, putting a hand on her back to push her toward the entrance of the cave. "Hunt good."

~

The hunting party had returned with an animal twice as large as those deer they'd killed before. Its carcass looked like a wildebeest—a very large one—and the excitement in the camp at this hunting success was plain to see.

The Kroo were already building a bonfire and gutting the animal when Rone and Lenna joined the others.

Since food obviously took priority over her, Rone went to join the others, and Lenna sat down next to Desh on the outskirts.

"They only kill one of these maybe once a year," Desh said, looking around at the excitement of everyone surrounding them. "It will feed the tribe for at least two weeks. That's why everyone is so happy."

Rone wasn't looking happy. He was frowning deeply as he was cutting meat off the body of the animal.

He looked like he wanted tear something apart.

Desh must have followed her eyes. "I told you before," he said matter-of-factly. "Women make the initial advances in this tribe."

Lenna's shoulders stiffened in surprise. "What do you mean?"

"I mean, a man isn't supposed to act until a woman has made the initial advance. That's how they know the woman is receptive. If a man acts before the woman has made herself available, it's a sign that he's weak."

"That disgusting Ugar gropes me any chance he gets."

"And everyone in this tribe knows him to be weak and a coward. Rone is neither of those things."

Lenna thought about this, turning her eyes back to Rone. He'd been watching her, but he looked away when their eyes met.

Desh gave an ironic laugh. "He's waiting for you to let him know you're interested. He can't make a move until you do."

"I thought you said he's never chosen a mate."

'He hasn't before. But what do you want to bet he does if you give him even the smallest sign you'd be receptive?"

Ridiculously, Lenna's heart started to race in excitement. She really shouldn't be so excited that this grumpy caveman was interested in her, but she was.

She really was.

She sat in silence as the meal was being prepared. Because the animal was so big, they made their normal big pot of stew, but they also roasted some of the meat on skewers.

It smelled delicious, and Lenna couldn't help but be pleased when Rone brought her over a big piece of roasted meat.

She smiled at him as she accepted it, and he gave her that same sober, watchful look.

When he returned to the fire for more food, Lenna pulled off a big chunk of her meat and handed it to Desh.

"He's not going to want you to give it to me," Desh said, eyeing the food longingly.

"I don't care. How long has it been since you've had any meat?"

"Ages." Desh snatched the meat and ate it in about five bites. "Thanks."

Lenna was still working on her skewer when Rone returned with more. He looked at the small amount she had left suspiciously, his eyes moving between her and Desh.

She gave him an innocent smile. "Food good."

His face relaxed. "Good." He handed her a second piece of meat, this time watching as she ate it.

She felt strange, embarrassed, almost shy—which was so weird because she just wasn't a shy sort of woman. She'd never had any problems letting a man know she was interested before. Just because she'd ended up with these cavemen didn't mean her nature would have changed.

But she couldn't seem to make the same sort of advance on Rone that she'd seen other women making, petting him, touching him intimately. It just felt too strange, too public.

She was feeling tense and uncomfortable when Rone finally scowled and walked away.

"Damn, Lenna," Desh muttered. "Put the poor guy out of his misery."

"He's not in misery."

"He's practically turning backflips to get you to make a move on him."

"He is not. He just gave me some meat. He hasn't done anything else."

"I've been here for three years. And I've never seen any man give a woman food if she wasn't already his mate, his previous mate, or his daughter. I'm telling you, it's the equivalent of backflips, and you're going to embarrass him in front of the tribe if you don't do something soon."

She suddenly felt guilty, on top of everything else. "Okay. Okay. Fine." She got up, but a stab of discomfort kept her from approaching Rone immediately.

She was Lenna. Completely independent, self-sufficient, reliant on no one. She wasn't sure she wanted to be some man's mate—so he could feed her, clothe her, take care of her.

It just wasn't who she was.

Instead of walking over to Rone, she moved out of the light of the fire so she could go to the bathroom in private.

This tribe didn't seem to be too concerned about privacy—although they only had sex in the dark and they did move to the periphery of the camp to relieve themselves, perhaps for sanitary reasons.

She refused to go the bathroom in front of other people, though, so she always found a convenient tree to hide behind.

She was coming back, still in the dark, when someone grabbed her.

She made a stifled cry of surprise as she threw out an elbow, connecting with a man's gut.

She could tell from the smell and sound of him that he was Ugar, groping at her again. The creep just wouldn't give up.

She elbowed him a second time, causing him to double over.

Hurrying back toward the fire, she heard him exclaim angrily and come after her.

He was stronger than her, but she'd been protecting herself from creeps all of her life, and she was confident of her ability to keep him off her. She was breathless, but more angry than afraid.

Disgusting asshole. The Kroo were right that his coming at her like this was weak and cowardly—a sign he wasn't really a man at all.

Before she could kick out at him, someone else was approaching, and two strong arms were picking Ugar up and throwing him several feet, so he landed with a painful thump against a tree.

Ugar whimpered and didn't try to move.

Lenna turned in astonishment to face Rone.

The first time Ugar had groped for her, Rone had laughed, thought it was funny. He'd laughed the second time too, the night after she'd arrived. This time, he'd attacked, tossing Ugar around in a way that must have really hurt him.

Lenna was flushed and panting and in a strange, excited daze as she stared up at Rone.

Rone had taken her shoulders in his hands and was studying her closely from head to foot, obviously checking to make sure she was all right.

"Good," she gasped, wishing she had a better grasp of the language. "Good. Lenna no want Ugar."

"No Ugar," Rone muttered, his eyes finally returning to her face with a strange sort of urgency.

"Lenna no want Ugar," she repeated, suddenly knowing exactly what she wanted to happen. She put a hand on his chest. "Lenna want Rone."

Rone made a throaty sound and grew still for a moment, his eyes still devouring her face.

"Lenna want Rone," she said again, stroking from his chest up to his shoulder. Every part of him was big and hard and masculine.

He groaned low and long, and then he grabbed her, swinging her up into his arms and carrying her toward the cave.

The rest of the tribe was still around the fire, eating and talking and celebrating a great kill. But Rone carried Lenna into the cave and then to his bed, laying her down on his pile of animal skins before moving above her.

He didn't kiss her. She hadn't seen anyone in the tribe really kiss. Instead, he rubbed his face against hers and then kept rubbing it down her body as he took off her clothes. His beard was thick and scratchy, and it felt to her like he was trying to cover her skin with his scent.

But it wasn't unpleasant. At all. Her heart was racing wildly and she kept rocking and clutching at him as he moved down her body. When he'd rubbed himself against every inch of her, he pulled apart her legs, kneeling between them.

Ridiculously, she was aroused. Her pussy throbbed achingly as he stared hotly at her completely naked body.

She was panting loudly as he lifted his tunic and freed his cock. He was big and hard and obviously just as turned on as she was. He grabbed her by the bottom and lifted her up so she was aligned with his erection. Then he guided himself inside.

He fucked her like that, on his knees, completely in control of her body, and she gasped and shook and couldn't tear her gaze away from his dark eyes as he took her.

She didn't come, but it was better than she ever could have imagined sex with a caveman like this could have been. She couldn't help but like how his face tightened up as he got closer, how his hips accelerated almost helplessly, how he groaned in pleasure as he came inside her, how his body relaxed afterwards and he collapsed beside her, breathing just as hard as she was.

She still had a few months left on her yearly birth control treatment, so she wouldn't have to worry about getting pregnant yet.

After a minute, Rone moved over her again, rubbing his face against her cheek and neck again, this time more gently.

She stroked his long, tangled hair, feeling irrationally pleased with him, with the whole situation.

He might be a grouchy, uncivilized, smelly caveman, but he was *her* caveman.

And she was now his mate.

FOUR

The next morning, Lenna woke up when Rone started to get out of bed.

She'd slept much more deeply than usual—partly because she was actually warm and partly because she genuinely felt safe, tucked between Rone and the wall of the cave.

She blinked several times, trying to clear her head, and she smiled when the first thing she saw was Rone's hairy face and sober eyes peering down at her.

He actually smiled back, if she read his expression correctly beneath his beard.

He said something, but her brain was still too fuzzy to interpret it.

At her questioning look, he repeated, "Rone... mate."

She sat up when she realized he was trying to confirm that she knew the significance of their having sex and sleeping together in his bed. "Yes. Rone mate."

He nodded and exhaled, like he was relieved. Then he reached down, took her arms, and pulled her to her feet. He scanned her body carefully, but he didn't seem to be ogling her. She wasn't sure what he was looking at exactly.

He said something, but the only word she understood was the final one. "...winter."

She shrugged. "Winter," she repeated.

He frowned in that way he did when she wasn't understanding what he was saying. "Cold. Winter."

"Yes. Cold winter." It was already quite cool outside, even in the warmest part of the afternoon. She was scared to think of how cold this planet would get when winter came for real. At least she wouldn't have to be sleeping on the ground without a blanket. "Bed good."

He frowned at her again, but evidently gave up trying to make her understand his point. He just turned around and headed out of the cave.

When she glanced back at the rest of the cave, she saw that several of the others were peering in her direction. They were looking at her differently now—some with respect and others, mostly the young women who didn't yet have mates, with resentment.

Evidently getting a man suddenly meant you mattered in the world of this tribe.

Shrugging off the stares, she leaned over to straighten up the blankets on Rone's bed before she headed out to breakfast.

Breakfast should have been good, since she sat next to Rone, he gave her a good meal, and some of the other women actually spoke to her. None of the women had said a word to her since she'd arrived, but having Rone as a mate evidently jumped her up high enough in the tribe's hierarchy for her to be addressed as an equal by other women.

It all felt strange, though—like this wasn't really her. It felt wrong on the deepest levels for her to be so pleased that a man had actually given her the social status she'd lacked before.

She'd never been that kind of person. She'd always been fiercely independent.

She might be stranded on this backwards planet, but she didn't want to turn into someone she wasn't.

So she was feeling rattled and uncomfortable as the quick meal ended and people started to go their separate ways—some to fish, some to gather roots, some to work on beating out animal hides, and some to other random tasks that were necessary for the tribe's survival.

Because she now had a mate, Lenna probably could have joined some of the other women who were mending clothes and cleaning the tools and weapons of their men. She needed to learn how to do those things, if she was going to take care of Rone the way she was expected to.

Something inside her resisted it, though. She wasn't used to taking care of anyone except herself. So instead of joining the women, she went to join Desh who was dealing with the bones of the wildebeest, whose carcass had been completely skinned, gutted, and carved up last night.

"You don't have to do this kind of stuff now," he said, when she crouched down beside him. "This is just for the fringes to do."

"I just spent the night with him. It doesn't completely change who I am."

"Yes, it does. He's going to get mad if he sees you doing this. He'll take it as an insult."

"He's already left camp for the day."

Desh just shook his head with a wry chuckle and didn't argue anymore. "This is an ugly job. Don't say I didn't warn you."

It *was* an ugly job. They had to pick the bones clean of the remaining meat, separate them from the cartilage, and then boil them until they were spotless. Animal bones were always kept to be used for tools or building supplies. Every part of every animal killed was used for something.

She and Desh worked for hours, and when they were finally through, Lenna was exhausted and covered with blood and animal innards. She wasn't a squeamish person by nature, but she felt rather sick when they finally laid the clean bones in the large pile at the back of the cave.

Desh was looking at her in faint amusement, but Lenna hadn't made one complaint all day. She couldn't let Desh say, "I told you so."

It was the middle of the afternoon, and the sun was bright and vibrant. Deciding it was warm enough, Lenna went down river until she found a private spot. There, she got into the water to clean herself off, still wearing her tattered clothes.

The tribe wasn't much in the habit of bathing—except when it was hot and they needed to cool down. Lenna had grown accustomed to being dirty and smelly, but she wasn't going to stay covered with animal guts.

She felt better when she got out, although she was shivering in the cool air. She wrung out her wet hair and finger combed it as she stood in the sun and tried to dry off.

When her skin was dry and her clothes were just barely damp, she started back toward the camp. It wasn't really smart to be by herself for very long. She was too close to camp to be in danger from another tribe—she was still in Kroo territory and no other tribe would violate that—but there could be predatory animals around.

Humans were clearly at the top of the food chain on this planet, and even the large bears and wolves wouldn't attack a group of humans under normal circumstances. But they might see her as vulnerable, out here by herself. She didn't want to risk it.

She'd only walked a few feet when she was suddenly confronted with a scowling Rone. He grunted out a bad-tempered question that included the words, "Lenna" and "danger."

She was startled and unsettled by his sudden appearance, and she didn't appreciate his attitude. She scowled back. "Lenna no danger. Lenna clean."

"Clean?" He looked around, obviously searching for something she'd been cleaning.

"Clean Lenna." She showed him her clean hands and clean hair.

Instead of relaxing, now that he'd understood what she'd been doing, his frown deepened even more. He grabbed her hands with both of his and pulled them up to his face, sniffing at them.

She let him do so, since smelling her hands was harmless enough, and he appeared genuinely upset about something. He sniffed up her arms and grabbed a handful her hair, sniffing at it too.

She gave a pained exclamation when he yanked her hair too hard. "Rone hurt Lenna!"

He immediately released her hair, which was a relief. He'd never seemed like a violent man or someone who would hurt her, and she was glad becoming his mate hadn't changed that.

He took her hands again and smelled them. "Lenna Rone mate," he said. "Rone mate."

"Yes. Yes." She was feeling bad now since he seemed so troubled. "Lenna Rone mate."

He rubbed his face and beard all over her hands and forearms, like he was trying to get her to smell like him again. "Rone mate. No... wildebeest. No... danger."

She didn't understand all of his words, but she realized now what he was saying, what had upset him.

He'd been worried about her when he'd returned to the camp and found out she'd wandered off alone. And then he must have smelled the wildebeest on her skin and realized what she'd been doing that morning.

Desh had said he'd be insulted if she did demeaning tasks—when as his mate she didn't have to. She might have rebelled against such an attitude, such a claim on her.

But he wasn't really insulted at all. He was upset. He was taking it as a sign that she didn't really want to be his mate after all.

Lenna's chest hurt very strangely at the knowledge. "Sorry. Sorry. Lenna Rone mate."

He was relaxing now. She could see it in his eyes, in the set of his shoulders. He was still rubbing his rough jaw against the inside of one of her wrists. "Lenna Rone mate," he murmured.

Ridiculously, she felt a little touched by his earnestness. "Yes. Yes."

She wasn't used to feeling guilty, and she didn't really like it. But she was part of this world—whether she wanted to be or not—and it wasn't right for her to defy the rules if it meant hurting Rone in the process.

She was going to have to learn how to act like his mate.

The next day, Rone gave her some lovely, soft animal skins to make herself a new outfit for the winter—because, as he explained, her torn clothes would be too cold. She had no idea how to do it, so she had to ask one of the other women for help.

She asked Mara, Tamen's second mate. She was a quiet, competent woman and had always looked at Lenna with interest rather than condescension or resentment, even before she was allowed to speak to her.

The next few days, Lenna spent learning how to sew clothes with the primitive supplies they had available, and she was very pleased with her new outfit—belted top and loose trousers—when she was finally finished.

The next afternoon, Mara came to her with a flint comb, a sharp instrument like a single-edged knife, and a clay bowl of oil. "Mate groom," she said, very seriously. "Lenna groom Rone."

Lenna's lips parted as she stared down at the grooming implements. Of course, she needed to groom Rone. That was what women did for their mates. She hadn't even thought about it, since she was so used to seeing Rone dirty and hairy.

But it would cast a negative light on him—on both of them—if she didn't do her job.

She'd watched plenty of women grooming their men in the cave. She knew how it was done. Comb and braid their hair. Shave their beard. Rub their skin with something like olive oil. Lenna was certainly capable of doing that for Rone.

She smiled at Mara and accepted the supplies. Then she went to find Rone.

She knew where he was. Since the tribe was still living off the meat from the wildebeest, the men hadn't left for another hunting party yet. Rone was down by the river today, spearing fish. He always came back with a large basket of them every day, which they dried and kept for the winter.

If she understood correctly, in the worst part of the winter, it was too cold to even leave the cave, so they had to save enough food to get them through that month.

When she found Rone, she stood and watched him for a minute. He was focused intently on the river, standing on the bank with his spear in his hand. Like everyone else, he'd changed to wearing trousers now that the weather was cooler, so nearly every part of his body was covered with either hair or animal skins.

Despite his appearance, she felt a little clench of ownership at the sight of him—and then felt a little embarrassed for feeling that way.

Remembering her purpose, she walked toward him.

He must have smelled or heard her before he saw her because he suddenly turned in her direction. He lowered his spear and waited until she reached him.

His eyes had moved from her head to her toes, and they focused on the supplies she was carrying. He lifted his gaze to meet hers. "Groom?" he asked, very seriously.

She nodded, telling herself there was no reason to feel so self-conscious. This was what she was supposed to be doing. "Groom," she repeated, just as soberly.

Couples could groom anywhere evidently—some did it in the cave and some outside, some in the evenings and some in the middle of the day. Tamen was across the river from them, and he was watching them curiously.

Lenna didn't want to make her first attempt at grooming where everyone else could see her, so she took Rone by the hand and led him farther down the river to where she'd bathed earlier that week.

It was private here, and there was a large flat rock that Rone could sit on.

He hadn't said a word since he'd asked the one question, but his dark eyes never left her face as she gestured for him to sit down. She felt irrationally nervous as she set down the bowl of oil and the blade on the ground and turned the comb in her hand. The teeth were thick and wide apart, which was a good thing. There was no way she could have gotten a fine-toothed comb through Rone's thick, tangled hair.

Taking a deep breath, she started to comb out his hair. It wasn't an easy task. She tried to do it carefully, rather than yanking at all the tangles, but sometimes it was impossible to be gentle and still get the knots out. She worked on it for almost an hour, and Rone sat wordlessly the whole time. Finally, she could get the comb all the way down his straight dark hair, so long it reached halfway down his back. She took some of the oil and slicked his hair down before braiding it in one long, tight braid down his back, tying it off with a short, thin cord.

"Good," she said, letting out a relieved breath at how nice his hair finally looked. It looked just as good as any other man's in the tribe—just as good as Tamen's. No one was going to look down on Rone for her grooming job.

"Good," Rone repeated, reaching up to feel his hair gently.

Now that his hair was done, she had to move on to his beard. It was a little easier, though, since she could take the sharp implement and just chop the length of it off section by section. Only when it was short enough to shave him did she start being careful. She'd never shaved someone else before—certainly not with such a primitive tool. She went very slowly, and gradually the thick hair on his face disappeared to reveal of square-chinned, high cheekboned, very handsome face.

She'd had no idea he would be so handsome beneath all the hair.

She rubbed oil into his face when she'd finished, feeling like she was looking at a stranger.

He must have felt that way too because he kept reaching up to touch his jaw and cheeks.

"Good," she said with a smile, pleased with her handiwork and hoping Rone would be pleased too.

He smiled back at her. "Good. Groom good."

To her surprise, she felt herself flushing a little at this praise.

There wasn't much left to do now. She had to oil the rest of his skin. She took off his clothes, secretly pleased with the look of his big, masculine body. He had a lot of hair on his chest, arms and legs, but it wasn't at all unpleasant.

What she really wanted was for him to get into the river to wash off, but he would probably take that as an insult. Instead, she took a piece of her old top, which she'd kept in case she needed cloth for some reason. She dipped it into the water and used it to wipe off the dirt from his body, rinsing and rewetting it several times before she was finished.

Then she took the oil, slicked up her hands, and rubbed it into his skin, starting with his arms, then moving to his chest, back, belly and legs.

She experienced the strangest surge of pleasure and possessiveness, as if grooming him had made him hers in a way he hadn't been before.

She was on her knees in front of him when she finally finished, and she looked up and met his eyes.

They were so hot her breath caught in her throat.

Her gaze immediately dipped down to his groin, and she could see that he was hard. Very hard. Completely erect.

They had sex in bed every night before they went to sleep. Lenna generally enjoyed it, although they always used the same position—that and doggie style seemed to be the only positions this tribe even knew—and it never lasted long enough for her to come.

She didn't resent it. She doubted Rone even knew that women were capable of reaching orgasm, and a cave, surrounded by so many other people, was not a place where Lenna would be comfortable teaching him otherwise.

He was never rough, and he was always pleased and appreciative afterwards, so she had no complaints at all.

But she felt a sharp pang of desire and possessiveness as she saw how hard he was at the moment.

Rone was a good mate. And a decent man. And her life here would have been so much harder without him.

She wanted to do something nice for him. She wanted to really please him.

So she reached for his erection.

Clearly confused, Rone grabbed her hands before she touched him.

She smiled up at him. "Good," she said, having no other vocabulary to let him know what she was doing. "Good."

He frowned, but he released her hands and stared down at her while she took his cock in her hands.

He sucked in a sharp breath as she ran her fingertips down the length of him and his body started to tighten.

She raised herself up on her knees and adjusted his position slightly until she could reach him with her mouth. She ran her tongue down the length of him, the way she'd done with her fingers.

He grunted softly, his thighs tensing palpably on either side of her.

She straightened up and smiled up at him. "Good."

"Good," he said thickly.

Her pussy throbbing even more, she leaned back down so she could take him fully in her mouth, pleased when he groaned helplessly.

She took a minute to establish a rhythm with her hand wrapped around the base of him and her mouth on his head, but then she applied hard, even suction to his cock.

Rone was losing it quickly, grunting out, "Good," over and over again as his body started to shake. He was gripping a fistful of her hair and getting louder and louder as he fell completely out of control.

He came with a long bellow, his body shuddering helplessly and his cock pulsing intensely as he released himself into her mouth.

When she finally straightened up, he'd almost collapsed onto the rock with a look of completely sated astonishment.

"Good," he gasped, as he was clearly trying to get his breath. "Good... thing."

She wasn't exactly sure what the last word was, but she'd always understood it to be a general, inclusive word like "thing."

She decided "good thing" was a reasonable enough way to describe a blow job.

She laughed and gently stroked his thighs.

He pulled her up so she was beside him on the rock. "Good mate," he said, stroking her hair. "Good thing. Lenna good mate."

She couldn't help but smile and feel rather proud of herself. She leaned over to press a kiss just to the side of his mouth, amazed that his face was so smooth and his expression so easy to see.

It was different, unnerving, but she was starting to like him clean-shaven like this.

He gave a little jerk and stared at her in confusion, and she realized he didn't know what a kiss was.

After a minute, he turned the same side of his face toward her again and waited. Chuckling, she leaned over and kissed him again.

"Good thing," he murmured again.
She couldn't disagree.

FIVE

A few weeks later, Lenna stayed up most of the night helping Mara as Tamen's current mate had a stillborn baby.

The woman's name was Jin, and she'd never been friendly with Lenna. In fact, she acted cool and superior with her, despite the fact that Lenna was Rone's mate, and Rone was capable of challenging the tribe's alpha.

Jin had been visibly pregnant since Lenna had arrived on the planet. She must have been at least seven months along. When she went into labor that evening, Lenna suspected that it was too early, and the rest of the women appeared to understand the same thing.

No one was excited, but no one seemed particularly upset. Mostly, the mood of the cave was tired and subdued, as Jin went through hours of labor to give birth to a very premature baby who was obviously dead.

It was very late—after midnight—when Lenna finally was able to go to bed. She was shaky and nauseated and deeply disturbed that the men and children had just slept through the whole thing and the women, even gentle Mara, had gone through the process as if it were just a normal event.

The Kroo didn't have very many babies. There were currently only two children under three. This should have been a loss. A personal loss for Tamen and Jin, and a loss for the tribe as a whole.

But Lenna was the only one who seemed genuinely upset by it. She'd never been particularly maternal or domestic. She'd never wanted to have children. But she also never wanted to again live through anything like what she had tonight.

She was shuddering helplessly as she crawled under the blankets beside Rone. He'd been asleep—like all the other men—but he woke up when she climbed over him to get into her normal position.

"Lenna," he mumbled, as she pulled the furs up over them both.

He sounded so warm and sleepy and familiar that something broke inside her. She choked on a sob and huddled against him, trying desperately not to cry.

Jin hadn't even cried over losing the baby. There was no reason for Lenna to do so.

Rone gave a questioning grunt and nuzzled at her face. It just made her shake even harder.

He propped himself up over her, trying to peer at her in the dark. "Lenna hurt?" This thought must have pushed him into urgency because he pulled back the covers and started to examine her body, evidently searching for injury or illness.

Lenna pushed him away, still strangling on suppressed tears. "Lenna no hurt."

Rone relaxed and sniffed at her face again where a couple of tears had streamed down her cheeks.

She wanted to explain, since he appeared genuinely concerned, but she realized she had no idea what the word in their language was for "sad." She'd been with them for more than two months now, and it had never come up.

It bothered her. A lot. That no one had needed to use the word sad in all that time.

There was something inhuman about it.

Rone was still sniffing her, and it made her feel even worse. She gently pushed him away and turned onto her side, her back to him. "Lenna sleep."

If a little part of her wanted Rone to be concerned enough to keep asking her what was wrong, it was to be disappointed. He relaxed behind her and mumbled, "Lenna sleep." He stroked her hair a few times. "Lenna good."

Lenna wasn't good. She was aching and queasy and so upset she was starting to go numb from it.

But evidently there was no one in this cave who could understand.

~

The next morning, she still felt sick and sad—even more so since everyone got up and went about their business as if nothing unusual had happened the night before.

Lenna found Desh after breakfast, desperately needing to speak to someone who might possibly comprehend how troubled she felt.

He was cleaning off the turnip-roots that had been picked the day before, so they could be added to the tribe's store for winter, but he looked up when Lenna sat down beside him.

"Does no one in this tribe even have a heart?" she asked, without preface or segue.

He evidently knew what she referred to. "Most of the babies they have die, either in miscarriages or when they're infants. They don't get attached the way we're used to. They can't get attached—not until there's a good chance the baby will live."

"I understand not acting like babies are the center of the universe, but they don't even seem to be upset about it. It's unnatural."

"Unnatural? They don't act like what we're used to, but how do you know how they're really feeling inside?"

The words caught her off-guard, and she had to nod in acknowledgement. It wasn't fair to judge the Kroo by her standards. After all, she didn't really know them at all.

In a milder tone, she asked, "Have you seem them after an adult dies?"

"Yes. They mourn. But they have to keep going about life, or they won't survive." He gave her a sympathetic look. "*We* won't survive. You're one of them now."

She shook her head. "No. I don't really think I am."

"You seem to be getting along pretty well with Rone."

"I guess. He seems to be the best of the group. But even he doesn't…doesn't seem to understand me." The thought made her uncomfortable—strangely guilty—so she decided to change the subject. "What about you? When are you going to choose a mate?"

Desh arched his eyebrows. "Have you seen any girls who seem interested?"

She hadn't. Desh was a handsome, fit young man, but he was definitely on the fringes of the tribe's society. "Why don't you go hunting with the men? If you killed a few animals, they'd probably be impressed."

"Have you ever tried killing an animal with a spear? It's not as easy as you think. These men have been practicing all their lives to do it."

Of course. There was no way she could expect a man who'd grown up with laser guns to be competent with a spear made of wood and stone. And Desh had evidently been always bookish—a real nerd, he'd called himself once. "Sorry," she murmured. "It was stupid of me to even ask."

"No. It wasn't stupid. I've been working on it in what little spare time I have. I think eventually I'll be able to hunt. Then maybe things will change."

She smiled at him, feeling better, like she wasn't the only one who was an alien on this planet. "Here. I'll help you with these this morning, and then maybe you'll have time to practice this afternoon."

~

They worked on the turnips for a few hours, and they finished by early afternoon—so Lenna went with Desh to help him practice with the spear.

She even tried to throw it a few times herself and immediately realized how difficult it really was. She had excellent aim with a gun, and she was strong for a woman, but there was no way she could throw a spear in a way that actually reached and pierced an animal's body.

Desh had clearly been practicing though, and he came quite close a few times.

She'd been planning to clean Rone's bed this afternoon, but she changed her mind since spending time with Desh had cheered her up, made her feel more like her real self.

Late in the afternoon, they were sitting against a rock, and Desh was helping her add more words to her vocabulary. She was laughing over his frustration with her inability to pronounce the word for "child."

She jerked to a sudden silence when she realized that Rone was standing a few feet away, glaring at them.

His angry expression was unmistakable, and she automatically stood up, as did Desh.

"Rone search Lenna," he growled, taking a few steps so he was right in front of her.

There was no reason for Lenna to feel guilty or like she'd done anything wrong. She *hadn't* done anything wrong. "Lenna here." She pointed to the ground where she stood.

Rone's dark eyes narrowed as she looked between her and Desh. He reached out to pull Lenna toward him by her arm. "Lenna Rone mate."

She gasped and shook off his grip. "Yes. Rone *mate*. Lenna *talk* Desh."

"No." Rone took her by the arm again. "No talk Desh. Lenna *Rone* mate." He was so angry he was almost shaking with it.

Lenna's mouth fell open in absolute astonishment. Surely he couldn't be telling her that she wasn't allowed to even talk to another man.

She looked back at Desh, who had been standing silently.

Desh shook his head. "There's no sense in arguing. He's not going to understand. There's no word in their language for friend. You're either mate or you're tribe or you're stranger or you're enemy. They don't understand any other relationships."

"That's ridiculous," she snapped, glaring back at Rone. "I'm not going to just stop talking to you."

They'd been talking in the common language, which evidently outraged Rone even more. "No talk Desh. Desh walk." He pointed fiercely toward the cave, in what was a very clear sign for Desh to leave.

Desh shook his head. "Sorry, Lenna. I can't get in a fight with him—not if I want to stay with the tribe."

"I know. I'll talk to you later."

Rone made a low growling sound as they spoke in a language he couldn't understand, and he only fell silent when Desh was out of sight.

Then he took her by both of the shoulders, not gently. "Lenna *Rone* mate."

She pulled out of his grip and opened her mouth to argue, but there was no argument she could make. She was his mate, and Desh was right. Rone was never going to understand that Desh wasn't a threat to that.

A caveman was going to act like a caveman, and she was stupid to hope he might ever act differently.

So she didn't say anything at all. She just turned away from him and started to walk back toward the cave.

Rone fell in step with her, and he kept peering at her face, like he was trying to figure out what she was thinking.

It wasn't just a language barrier that was standing between them. They were from two completely different worlds.

Even if she had the words to explain her point of view to him, he was never going to understand.

~

She was still simmering with resentment and annoyance that evening. She was tired and upset and not hungry at all, so she didn't eat much dinner.

This clearly confused Rone, who kept trying to offer her more food—roasted meat, stew, bread, roots—but she just shook her head.

After her emotional upheaval the night before with the stillborn baby and her fight with Rone, she simply had no appetite at all.

She didn't stay up to listen to the storytelling or music that evening. She was exhausted so she went to bed early. She was still awake, however, when Rone came to bed an hour or so later.

When he got under the covers, he turned her over and started to rub his face against hers, the way he always did. It was his version of foreplay.

Under normal circumstances, she enjoyed it. Sometimes, he went slow enough to turn her on, and she appreciated that he was never rough or mean.

But there was absolutely no way she could have sex with him tonight. It wasn't that she was holding a grudge. It was that she was too upset to open up her body to him.

She gently pushed him away.

He gave an indignant huff and tried to move over her again.

"No," she said, keeping her voice soft so no one else in the cave could hear. She might be rejecting him, but she wasn't going to do it in front of the entire tribe. "No."

Frowning, he reached out to curve his big hand around the side of her ribs. "Lenna Rone mate."

"Yes, Lenna Rone mate. No fuck Rone." Their word for sex was harsh and crude sounding, so she always interpreted it as fuck rather than sex. She paused, searching her mind for one of the words Desh had taught her that afternoon. "No fuck Rone *now*."

She met his eyes, praying he'd understand. She knew she was walking a tightrope wire here. If Rone decided she wasn't a mate to him, he could very likely move on to someone else.

But she couldn't—she just couldn't—have sex with him right now.

He kept his hand on her ribs, but he didn't try to move over her again. "Lenna Rone mate," he said, very softly, his eyes searching her face.

"Yes," she murmured. "Lenna Rone mate."

He let out a breath and relaxed back onto the bed, his expression sober and confused.

She lay beside him, staring up at the ceiling of the cave, wondering how she had even gotten here.

A few months ago, she'd been on her own ship, doing a normal job, minding her own business—surrounded by a civilized world. Yes, the world was dominated by an oppressive regime, but at least she knew what to expect from people and she'd been dependent on no one.

She was dependent now. She was dependent on this man beside her.

And in the deepest, most important ways, she couldn't understand him at all.

~

The next morning, Rone left with a hunting party, so she had a temporary reprieve from him for two days.

At the end of the second day, the men returned in victory—having killed the largest animal she'd ever seen on the planet. It was twice the size of that wildebeest Rone had killed the previous month. It looked like a woolly rhinoceros.

Whatever it was, it was clear that the kill was a rare feat and a cause for great celebration.

They built a huge bonfire and feasted and laughed and blew on bone flutes. Some of them even got up and danced in front of the fire, which she'd never seen any of the Kroo do before.

They celebrated well into the night. Lenna tried very hard to act normal with Rone. She wasn't angry with him anymore, but she still felt strange and unsettled about him—like he was a stranger she was going through life with.

She hadn't felt that way about him before, so she tried to force herself back to normal, but it still seemed like she was just going through an act.

He appeared pleased that she ate and smiled and sat next to him, although every once in a while she'd catch him peering at her face in the firelight, like he was trying to read her mind.

The festivities were wilder than any she'd ever witnessed from the tribe before, and her eyes widened in shock when two of the young, unclaimed women took off their clothes to dance. They were very young. They couldn't have been more than sixteen years old.

She wasn't at all happy about the fact that Rone was watching them.

All the men were watching them. No one seemed to think it was strange. But Lenna didn't like it, so she got up on the pretense of relieving herself.

Mostly, she just wanted to get away for a few minutes. Hopefully, when she returned, the girls would have stopped dancing and put their clothes back on.

After all, it was cold tonight.

She waited several minutes, just on the outskirts of the firelight, and then she returned to the circle of the tribe. When she reached them, she jerked to a sudden stop, staring in astonishment at what was happening.

One of the young women—Sorel was her name, Tamen's daughter, who used to come on to him before he'd taken Lenna as a mate—was standing over Rone, stroking his hair, his face.

Rone. Lenna's mate. That shameless girl was all over him.

She knew objectively that this happened. Unless a woman had already been claimed as a mate, she was allowed to show interest to any man she wanted—even if the man was taken. After all, a man was allowed to move on to a new mate whenever he wanted.

Obviously, Sorel had decided she wanted Rone to move on, and she was making her play for him right there in front of the tribe, beautiful and nubile and naked.

And Rone was looking up at Sorel, doing absolutely nothing.

Nothing.

Not pushing her away. Not removing her hands from his face.

Nothing.

Lenna burned with outrage, astonishment, and something akin to betrayal.

Rone was supposed to be *her* mate.

Mara had been watching the proceedings with a frown on her face, and she was the first one to notice Lenna's return. She stiffened, looking between Rone and Lenna.

This evidently clued the rest of the tribe in because everyone looked over toward Lenna.

She stood there frozen, staring at Rone, whose eyes had moved in her direction. His back straightened up and his expression changed. He looked almost expectant.

She had no idea what she was supposed to do, but she couldn't believe that Rone wasn't pulling away from Sorel. Lenna was standing right there. The least he could do was feel shame for letting her touch him that way.

The swell of indignation and betrayal grew so intense in her chest, in her throat, that she couldn't even breathe. She made a choked sound, trying to open up her windpipe.

Rone still didn't move, although something was transforming in his expression as she stood motionless. In a different situation, she would have thought it was disappointment, but that couldn't be what she was seeing in him now.

Maybe he was tired of her. Maybe he wanted to move on to Sorel.

If he did, there was nothing she could do about it.

The truth hit her so hard she could barely control herself. She had to turn away, stumble toward the cave, so she wouldn't break down in front of everyone.

It didn't matter. It didn't *matter*. If Rone didn't want her anymore, then that was just fine. He would still be obliged to take care of her. She just wouldn't have to put up with his obnoxious peering and possessiveness anymore.

She hadn't even made it to the cave when she heard a voice behind her, but—to her disappointment—it wasn't Rone.

It was Desh.

"Damn it, Lenna," he muttered, "you've got to go back there right now."

"What are you talking about? Rone was the one getting felt up by another woman."

"Girls do that all the time." Desh looked unexpectedly urgent, far more urgent than she'd seen him before. He was breathless. He must have run to catch up to her. "That's what they do. But he's *your* mate, and if you don't act like you want him, then he's going to assume you don't care."

"What are you talking about?"

"He's *yours*, and someone else is trying to take him. You're okay with that?"

"No, I'm not okay with it." Her voice was hoarse, and she had to swipe away a stray tear, but she hadn't lost control. "But he's capable of controlling himself, you know."

"He hasn't done anything. He's done nothing but sit there and wait for you to come back. But right now he thinks you don't want him. That's what you told him by walking away."

"I don't—" She broke off, suddenly understanding that she'd completely misinterpreted everything. She'd been assuming these people acted like the people she was used to.

And they didn't.

She knew they didn't.

"You just told him—in front of the entire tribe—that you don't want him."

"I do want him," she breathed.

"So go show him that." Desh seemed to be hiding a smile now, but Lenna was too distracted to really notice.

She took a shaky breath, turned back around, and hurried toward the bonfire.

Everyone was still in roughly the same position. Sorel was still petting at Rone's hair, but he was hunched over, frowning down at the ground, rather than looking at her, and he briefly swatted away her hand, like she was pestering him but he wasn't sure what to do about it.

Lenna knew what to do.

She marched back into the circle of the tribe, and they all fell silent as she approached. Without pausing, she pushed Sorel away from Rone and she slapped the hands that had been touching him.

Not gently.

"No," Lenna said sharply, glaring coldly at Sorel. "Rone Lenna mate. No Sorel. *No Sorel.*"

A low murmur rippled out from the others in response to this, and Rone straightened up, his face transforming to something like awe as he gazed up at her.

Sorel made a face, and she glanced briefly down at Rone, as if to gauge his level of interest in her.

Rone didn't appear to be aware that Sorel existed in the world. He was smiling up at Lenna and reaching to pull her down beside him.

Lenna was pleased and proud and relieved—and a little bit embarrassed by the whole episode. But she couldn't regret anything when she saw that look in Rone's eyes.

She'd been stupid to doubt him. He obviously didn't want anyone for a mate but her.

He'd just been needing to see that she wanted him too.

∼

Later that evening, when they went to bed, she let Rone rub himself all over her body as he took her clothes off. She clung to him, stroked him eagerly. Then, for the first time, she pushed him onto his back and rose up over him.

He stared up at her, his eyes hot but his expression confused. When he tried to sit up, probably to get into his normal position on his knees between her legs, she held him down and straddled him.

He made a choked sound of pleasure as she took his cock in her hands. She held him between her palms as she leaned down over him and started to rub him all over, the way he'd always done her.

"Rone Lenna mate," she said, as she rubbed his chest with her cheek and jaw. "Rone Lenna mate."

"Yes. Yes. Lenna," he gasped, his big body tightening like a fist. "Lenna mate."

Her pussy, her whole body, was throbbing almost painfully, and she couldn't wait any longer. She lifted her hips enough to slide herself down over him, sheathing his cock with her body. Both of them moaned as she fit herself around him.

Rone arched his back and grabbed for the furs beneath them, obviously unused to this position. His eyes crawled from her flushed face and down to her bare breasts, and even lower to where they were joined as she started to ride him.

She was tight and wet around him, and she could already feel an orgasm coiling inside her. Her rhythm was fast and hard, causing her breasts to jiggle and her breath to come out in loud huffs.

Rone was grunting loudly as he lifted his hands to hold her by the ribs. He never closed his eyes. He never looked away from her.

Soon, she was so close she was almost sobbing with it. She moved one hand so she could rub her clit urgently.

The orgasm broke fast and hard, and she bit back a long, low groan as her body shook helplessly through the spasms. Rone was pretty far gone himself, but when her vision cleared she saw that his brow was lowered in that way it did when he was confused by something.

She kept riding him as her pussy clamped down around him even more tightly, and then he moved a hand to where hers had been, rubbing her the way she'd been doing to herself. She helped him find her clit and then moaned as he massaged it enthusiastically.

She came again, biting down hard on her lower lip as the pleasure overwhelmed her. She didn't want to be too loud.

They were surrounded by other people. It was dark, and no one paid much attention to other couples having sex, but still... women didn't normally scream during sex in this tribe.

Rone came with her this time, letting out a loud helpless sound as his hips jerked through his climax. She collapsed on top of him afterwards, breathless and deliciously sated.

He stroked her back and her hair, mumbling, "Rone mate. Rone mate."

She figured that, for him, this was an expression of affection. They didn't seem to have a word for love in this tribe, but at least this was close. She pressed a kiss on his shoulder, and then lifted her head so she could kiss him on the lips.

He still didn't seem to know what to do with kisses, but he smiled and ran his hand down her hair, holding his head in place like he wanted her to kiss him again.

She did. "Lenna mate," she told him, feeling flushed and sore and so much better than she had for the last few days.

Rone was different from what she was used to, but he wasn't as different as she'd thought.

SIX

A few weeks later, Lenna woke up shivering.

She was pressed up against the wall of the cave, clinging to a piece of animal skin that barely covered her body, and her teeth were chattering so hard it woke her up.

As she turned over, she knew what had happened. Rone must have rolled over and taken all the covers with him.

She tugged at the corner of animal skin as hard as she could, pulling enough to make Rone grunt and roll over onto his back. Then she scooted over closer to him so she could cover herself up and take advantage of the heat from his body.

It must be almost time for them to get up, but they'd had a major snow storm three days ago, and so they'd been stuck in the cave since then. A few of the men had dug their way out enough to dispose of waste, but no one else had left the cave in three days.

There was no sense in hurrying to get up this morning.

Her attempt to claim more covers woke Rone up. He was shifting beside her now and clearing his throat. Her teeth still chattering, she moved even closer to him, pleased when he rolled onto his side and wrapped his arms around her.

"Lenna cold," she whispered through her shivering.

"Lenna cold like ice." He tightened his arms, evidently concerned by the fact that she was shivering so intensely. "No good."

She'd finally learned enough of the language to realize that it did include similes, which was their primary method of describing feelings. "Rone stole blankets."

He huffed in amusement and rubbed her back and her arms for a few minutes until she finally stopped shivering.

When she was able to relax, she adjusted her position so she was lying more comfortably against him. Feeling a wave of familiarity and affection, she pressed a little kiss against his chest. "Lenna warm now. Glad Rone here."

He nuzzled her hair. "Glad Lenna here. Lenna *home*."

She'd never been exactly sure what the last word he said meant. She'd heard it only occasionally, and Desh had told her he thought it meant home.

Her chest and belly started to flutter in a very strange way at the words and the hoarseness of Rone's voice. No matter how much she appreciated him, it wasn't like she could really fall in love with him. She knew he was intelligent—probably the smartest man in this cave other than Desh—but his life, his world, was so much smaller, simpler, harsher than hers.

This just wasn't her home. She would always be a stranger here.

She'd known Rone for more than three months now—been his mate for more than two. And yet she still knew so little about him.

For some reason, this fact bothered her a lot, so she sorted through her vocabulary in her mind for a minute until she was able to ask, "Where cave Rone born?"

He turned his head to peer at her face, clearly surprised by the question.

She tried again, making sure she enunciated correctly, in case he hadn't understood. "Where cave Rone born?"

"No cave." He met her eyes and said a word she didn't understand.

She frowned and shook her head.

He repeated the word twice and lifted up the covers so they were tented above them in the bed.

That she understood. "Tent," she said, trying out the new word. "No cave. Tent."

He nodded. "Tribe no cave. Walk always. Follow herds. Sleep tents. Far distance."

This made sense to her. From the little she knew about hunter-gatherer societies, most were at least semi-nomadic, following their source of food as it migrated with the seasons.

Now that she thought about it, the Kroo must have prime real estate, to have access to food most of the year round in this one protected location.

"Rone glad cave?" she asked, wondering if he missed his old life, his old tribe. "Rone glad Kroo?"

"Yes. Rone glad cave. Rone glad Kroo." He let out a long breath. "Tribe Rone born… hard like stone." He patted his chest to make it clear where his old tribe had been hard. "Kroo good. Cave good. Lenna good."

She pressed another little kiss onto his chest, touched and amazed by this clear evidence that she was one of the reasons Rone was happy here.

"Lenna born cave?"

She shook her head.

"Tent?"

"No." She had to search for things in his world that she could compare an Earth city with. "Tent hard like stone. Big like mountain."

His eyes widened. "Where?"

"Farther sun. Near stars."

He was eyeing her soberly and with obvious astonishment. But he believed her. He might not understand the existence of a planet other than this one, but he believed her. "Lenna fall here?" he asked, very softly.

The words struck her strangely, causing an ache in her chest. Finally, she nodded. "Fall here."

He adjusted her against him so both of his arms were wrapped around her. "Lenna hurt?"

Ridiculously, her eyes were burning with emotion. She had no idea why. "Lenna good," she murmured.

"Lenna *home*."

She had no idea what to say to that, but she wouldn't have contradicted him for the world.

She tried to imagine a scenario in which she were somehow rescued from this planet and took Rone with her.

He would be so confused, so unhappy, so shaken to the core of his soul. His world was only as high as the sky over this planet, and it would be wrong for her to want him to be any other way.

This world wasn't a fall for him. He loved it, was proud of it, worked to make it the best he could for him, for her, and for his tribe.

If more people in the Coalition did the same, then the civilized universe would be far better than it was.

"Lenna hurt?" he asked, snuffling at her face, where a tear had slid out of her eyes.

"Lenna no hurt," she managed to say.

He rubbed his face against hers for a long time, until she couldn't help but feel better. After a few minutes, she smiled and stroked his long braid.

He smiled when she did, and he lowered his head again, nuzzling her neck and shoulders. She could feel the increasing tension in his body and was already getting a little turned on, but when he started to take off her top, she murmured, "Lenna cold."

He frowned at this predicament, but he improvised quickly by sliding his hands under the bottom of her top so he could rub her bare skin with his hands. He seemed to enjoy the way her nipples tightened under his touch because he kept tweaking and twirling them until Lena was squirming helplessly and moaning softly in pleasure.

Eventually, he lifted her shirt enough to rub his face against her belly, and she got more and more excited as his face moved closer to her groin. She clutched at the animal skins beneath her and tried to stifle her vocal responses.

Rone kept looking up at her face occasionally, obviously very pleased with his effect on her. When he slid off her loose trousers, he lowered his head so he could sniff at her pussy.

She was very wet, very turned on. He obviously could smell how much because he made an appreciative growl in his throat.

When he nuzzled at her arousal, she cried out and arched up.

"Lenna warm now?" he asked with a little smile.

It took her a minute to realize he was actually teasing her. "Lenna warm. Lenna good. Good, good."

He nuzzled her again until she couldn't help but grind herself against his face.

He grabbed one of her legs so he could hold her open. He knew where her clit was now. Ever since he'd watched her rub herself off during sex, he'd always tried to make her come. He seemed to get as much pleasure out of watching her come as coming himself. But he'd always used his hand.

He'd never done this before.

Parting her thighs to make room for his face, he rubbed her pussy with his face the way he always rubbed the rest of her body.

She bit her bottom lip and bucked up at the surge of pleasure. Then she totally lost it when he started to lick her with his tongue.

She came hard and long, unable to hold back the shameless moan as her head tossed back and forth on the bed.

When she'd finally relaxed, Rone rose up onto his knees, his face damp and his eyes hot and pleased.

"Good, good, good," she mumbled, unable to articulate any other word. She reached out for his cock, which was visibly hard beneath his animal skins.

"Rone fuck Lenna now?" he asked, sucking in a breath at her touch.

"Yes. Rone fuck Lenna. Good."

He turned her over onto her hands and knees and quickly freed his cock. Then he parted her cheeks and guided himself into her hot, wet pussy.

Both of them groaned at the penetration, and Lenna fisted her hands in the blankets beneath her at the tight, full feeling.

Rone took her hard and fast, leaning over behind her. She was surrounded by his strong body, his hot skin, his fast breathing. She was vaguely aware that they weren't alone. It was still dark in the cave, but those around them would obviously know what they were doing.

She didn't even care. She wanted them to know how hard Rone was taking her, how good he was making her feel.

She'd never felt this way in her life before, but she couldn't deny the feeling now.

He fucked her from behind until she came again, stifling her scream of pleasure in the blankets. Then he pulled out and turned her over. He was starting to kneel between her legs, but she pulled him down into missionary position so she could wrap her arms around him.

It took him a minute to figure out this new position, but he soon built up another fast, rough rhythm as she tightened her legs around him and pulled the blanket up to cover them.

He rubbed his face against hers as they moved together, and it felt like Lenna's heart would burst out of her chest. She held on to him tightly and gave herself over to the feeling, crying out uninhibitedly as he brought her to climax again just before he came himself.

Both of them were breathless and clingy afterwards. Rone kept nuzzling her cheek, her jaw, her shoulder, and he was mumbling words it took her a minute to hear clearly.

"Lenna good. Lenna home. Lenna *home*."

At least for the moment, it felt like she was.

A few days later, the snow finally melted enough for them to come out of the cave.

Lenna had spent most of her life on a space ship, so she wasn't inclined to get cabin fever. She was surprised, however, by how happy she was to see the sky again, the sun, the familiar trees near the cave, the mountains beyond them.

Everyone seemed excited, even though they had to trudge through the remaining snow. After breakfast, Mara and Lenna gathered up the bedding and carried it outside to clean, hanging it up afterwards on big bare branches to air out in the cold, fresh air.

They were laughing over the men's attempt to make holes in the ice to fish, and Lenna was hit with the strange realization that she really liked Mara.

Mara was gentle and intelligent, and she had a sense of humor. She never complained, even though she was a former mate of the tribe's leader, and therefore would never have a mate again. She had two sons. One had already left the tribe, as boys did when they hit puberty. The other must be almost twelve. Soon he would leave too, and she would never see him again.

Mara didn't seem sad about this fact. She was proud of her boy—proud that he would become a man soon who was capable of making it on his own.

Lenna could almost—almost—understand why his leaving wasn't a source of grief.

He couldn't stay here. Only weak men didn't leave the tribe they were born into, and no mother would want her son to be weak.

As she laughed with Mara, Lenna looked across the river to where Rone was carefully trying to carve out a hole in the ice. He glanced up, as if he sensed she was watching him, and their eyes met across the distance.

He smiled, and he was still smiling when he looked back down at the ice.

Lenna was still smiling too as she started back to the cave to get the rest of Rone's blankets from his bed.

Before she reached the cave entrance, a sound made her pause. It was a soft bleating, like a whimper, coming from behind a cluster of large rocks nearby.

She went to investigate and found a very young fawn—one of the deer-like animals that moved in herds and were the main source of food for the tribe.

It was tiny and sprawled out in the snow, crying helplessly.

Lenna ran toward it, kneeling down to see what was wrong. It tried to pull away from her instinctively, but its back right leg was obviously injured and half its tail was gone, clawed away in a raw gash.

A predator—maybe one of those wolves—had obviously attacked it. Lenna didn't know how it had gotten away, unless the wolf had caught its mother and been too distracted to follow it.

Either way, she couldn't just leave it here. The poor little thing was helpless. It would freeze or starve to death, and it might attract predators, which they didn't want lurking around the cave.

She gathered it up into her arms. It fought her, of course, but it wasn't strong enough to get away. Eventually, it went limp, its big dark eyes staring up at her pitifully.

She brought it into the cave and was using medicinal herbs on its injury when Mara came in.

"Deer hurt," Lenna said, when the other woman stared at her in amazement.

Mara shook her head. "Deer young. No eat." They only hunted mature animals—never the very young.

Lenna was horrified about the idea of eating this poor little thing. "No eat. Hurt. Baby. Stay here."

Mara's eyes widened in astonishment. "No stay. Deer. No baby."

Since Lenna didn't know how to argue with a worldview that saw animals as nothing but food, she just shrugged and kept tending the deer. After she'd worked on its wounds, she tried a variety of vegetables until she found a couple that the deer would eat.

After a while, Rone came in, and Lenna realized that Mara must have gone to get him to let him know his mate was doing something very strange.

Rone crouched down beside where Lenna was sitting. "Deer no stay."

"Deer stay," Lenna said matter-of-factly. She knew they would think this was bizarre, so she wasn't going to get angry. But she wasn't going to let this poor little animal die.

It needed her. It already seemed to trust her, nuzzling her hand gently, maybe looking for more to eat.

"No food," Rone said, pushing Lenna's hand away from the deer. "Winter."

She frowned at him, realizing he was worried that they couldn't spare food for an animal during the winter. "Deer eat Lenna food. Deer stay. Baby." She stroked the soft fur. "Baby. Stay here until no hurt."

Rone shook his head, looking between the deer and Lenna helplessly. Then he finally shrugged and stood up. "Lenna no obey Rone."

Her eyes shot up with a surge of indignation, but when she saw his face she realized he was amused by her stubbornness rather than annoyed. She smiled at him. "Lenna no obey Rone."

~

So for the next two weeks, Lenna took care of the injured fawn. Fortunately, the weather was decent—cold but not snowing—so she was able to go outside and forage for food for the animal without using up the tribe's store.

Slowly, the fawn started to heal, and soon it could walk with a limp. It seemed to have grown quite attached to Lenna, and she loved the way it would nestle against her. She knew the rest of the tribe thought she was crazy for caring for an animal, but as long as she cleaned up after it and didn't waste their food on it, no one complained.

But eventually it snowed heavily again, and once again the tribe was trapped in the cave, unable to get outside. Lenna gave the fawn half of her own share of food, but she knew some of the others—namely Tamen—were bristling with indignation at the waste.

Whenever Tamen started to object, however, Rone stood between them.

Tamen might be the lead alpha of the tribe, but Rone wasn't letting anyone act against his mate.

A few days into the snowstorm, however, Rone was outside digging out a path. It was almost mealtime, and Tamen came over to where Lenna was sitting on the bed, stroking the fawn beside her.

"No good food," he said, looking down at her stonily. "Eat deer."

"No!" she gasped, pulling the animal closer to her. "Deer baby."

"Deer *food*." Tamen's face was as cold as ice. He'd obviously been bristling about this for a while, and he was using Rone's absence to make his move.

"No!" Lenna scrambled up, picking up the deer and hurrying away from Tamen, toward the entrance of the cave. "Rone, Rone!"

Tamen kept advancing, however, and Rone didn't make an appearance. He must be too far away to hear her.

She wasn't strong enough to stop him, and there was no one in this cave who would help her. Or *could* help her. Mara was looking at her with obvious sympathy, but also fear. If she tried to challenge Tamen, she would have no one to take care of her.

Lenna couldn't blame her for not taking that risk.

Not over a deer.

This tribe didn't understand pets. It only understood nature. Animals were food or for leaving alone. You didn't bring one into the household.

"Rone!" Lenna called again, trapped between Tamen and the icy cold outside the cave.

He still didn't hear her.

Tamen was about to reach for the deer when Desh was suddenly beside her. He grabbed the fawn from Lenna's hands and stepped outside with it.

When he returned, the deer was no longer in his arms.

"Desh!" Lenna gasped, speaking their common language. "What did you do?"

"I'm really sorry, but it was the only thing to do. I let it go outside. If you kept it any longer, Tamen would have killed it. And if Rone comes back, you're risking a civil war in the tribe. You don't want that, do you?"

Of course she didn't want that. It would have been wrong to put Rone in that position. Desh was right, of course.

But that poor little deer, all by itself in the cold.

Her eyes were burning as she looked back at Tamen, resenting him more than she ever had before.

"Deer young," Desh said firmly. "No eat. Gone now."

Tamen's eyes narrowed at this act of defiance from someone on the fringes, but he didn't argue. He just turned his back and returned to his side of the cave.

Lenna stood shaking, staring out into the dark.

"Just let it go, Lenna. I'm really sorry."

She nodded at Desh, reaching out to touch him lightly before he walked away.

She knew he was right. She had to let it go. But she couldn't stop herself from stepping outside just to see if she could see it.

It was so cold and the wind was so strong she could barely breathe, and she couldn't see a thing past the swirling snow.

Her little deer was going to die out here.

"Lenna!" a rough voice came from nearby, nearly drowned out by the wind.

Before she could turn around, a big man had approached her and picked her up bodily, tossing her over his shoulder to carry her back inside.

Rone.

It was Rone.

He carried her over to his bed and wrapped his arms around her, obviously trying to get her warm again. "Cold danger," he said roughly. "No leave cave. No leave cave."

Her teeth were chattering, and she was still close to tears. She did her best to explain to Rone what had happened.

When Rone understood, he sucked in a breath and stood up, turning toward Tamen with a glare colder than she'd ever seen on his face before.

Remembering Desh's words, she grabbed for his leg, which was the only part of him she could reach. "No. Rone no. Stay with Lenna. Stay."

For a moment, she wasn't sure what he was going to do, but he eventually relented and lowered himself into the bed with her. They were sitting up, their backs against the wall, and he wrapped both of his arms around her. "Lenna lost deer," he muttered. "Lenna deer home."

She almost cried because it was so clear that Rone understood this was a loss for her. He might not have ever seen someone treat an animal this way, but he understood her.

He cared about her.

She managed to control herself as she shuddered in his embrace. "Lenna good."

"No." He stroked her hair. "Lenna hurt."

She was hurt. Her poor little baby deer was probably dying right now out there in the snow.

But she couldn't let Rone get into a real fight with Tamen. The two men were evenly matched. There was no telling who would win such a fight. She couldn't take that risk. What if Tamen would seriously injure Rone? What if he would kill him?

There was absolutely no way she would let that happen.

And at least Rone knew she was sad.

It meant something—that he understood.

SEVEN

"So does Rone know you came out with me this afternoon?" Desh asked, the brisk wind blowing his hair back and the bright sun burnishing it almost golden.

Lenna made a face at him. "We have an understanding."

"And is the understanding that you don't tell him when you hang out with me and he doesn't get angry about it?" Desh's mouth twitched just slightly.

Lenna couldn't help but laugh. Rone was away from the cave all day, hunting small animals now that the snow had finally melted and the weather started to warm up. She tried to respect Rone's worldview and so made a point of not spending too much time with Desh, since she didn't want Rone to get jealous or confused. But Desh wasn't any sort of threat to her relationship to Rone.

Desh was her friend. She had few enough as it was, and she wasn't going to lose him.

So when he'd told her he was going out this afternoon to practice hunting, she'd decided to go with him. After being trapped for the month of winter, she wanted to get out in the sunshine and stretch her legs anyway.

The big herds of grazers wouldn't start coming back through this area for another several weeks, but the small mammals were beginning to come out of hiding, now that the weather had turned. So far, Desh had come close to killing two of them—but each time he had missed.

She took a deep breath. "It almost smells like spring."

"It's still pretty cold to call it spring yet."

"I know. But you can smell soil and…and something almost warm. That smells like spring to me."

"How does a city girl like you even know what spring smells like?"

She slanted her eyes over at Desh and saw that he was smiling. "Even on Earth, you can still smell it occasionally."

For some reason, the words hit her strangely—poignant, almost nostalgic. She didn't miss Earth. Not at all. She hadn't lived there since she was fifteen. After her parents had died, she'd stowed away on a merchant ship and had only returned to Earth a handful of times since.

She wasn't sure exactly what had caused the clench in her chest, but the feeling mingled into the cold smell of spring as she kept inhaling.

Desh was quiet for a minute, as if he were sensing something similar. Then he put his finger to his lips in the universal signal for quiet and nodded over to her right.

She looked in the direction he indicated and gasped softly when she saw five deer grazing in the distance. They were obviously not part of one of the big herds—maybe just stragglers who'd gotten left behind for the winter.

Desh started to poise his spear when Lenna noticed that the smallest one didn't have a tail and had a visible scar on its back flank.

"Wait!" she exclaimed under her breath, reaching over to put a hand on his arm. "Don't! Look at the young one. It think it's my little baby deer."

"It couldn't be," Desh murmured, lowering his spear.

Very slowly, they took a step closer, and Lenna's heart jumped as she recognized the markings on the fur and the shape of the scar.

"It is!" she gasped. "I can't believe the little guy made it!" She was so astonished and happy that she was ridiculously close to tears. "Please don't kill him."

"Of course I won't. But can I try for one of the other ones? If I bring back a deer at this time of year, I think they might finally accept me as a real man."

She actually didn't like the idea of his killing any of the deer, now that she'd gotten to know the fawn. But it would be completely irrational for her to insist that Desh not do what was obviously in the best interests of him and the entire tribe, who could really use the food.

So she nodded, and both of them slowly stalked over toward the group of deer. She thought they were completely silent, but three of the deer raised their heads suddenly, their ears perked and their eyes wide.

The oldest one bounded off in a run when it saw them approaching, and the others followed. For just a moment, Lenna thought maybe the baby had recognized her. It stared at her for longer than the others and didn't move right away.

But it was probably wishful thinking on her part. Soon, the fawn was joining the others in fleeing.

Lenna and Desh ran after them, coming over a rise to see a long stretch of cold, dead grassland before them. There were several more deer there, and they joined together as they ran away from Lenna and Desh.

Desh pulled to a stop. "We better stop chasing them or they'll never stop running. Let's just head in that direction more slowly and maybe we can catch one unaware."

So they caught their breaths and followed more slowly. Soon the deer were out of sight, but Lenna knew they'd stop running when they thought they were safe.

If she secretly hoped she and Desh wouldn't catch up to them, she certainly didn't say as much.

They walked for almost an hour, occasionally catching sight of the deer in the distance, and eventually they were farther away from the cave than Lenna had been since she'd arrived.

Looking around for the first time, she stopped and put a hand out to touch Desh's arm. "Wait. Do you know where we are?"

"We're still in no-man's land. I'd know if we entered another tribe's territory."

"I know, but isn't that the forbidden mountain?" She gestured to the next mountain over, where there was a familiar peak higher than the others.

None of the mountains on this planet were very high. Compared to some of the mountains on earth, these would barely be classified as hills.

Desh nodded, breathing heavily. "Damn. It is. I hadn't realized we'd gotten so far."

"Look," she said, pointing over to the foot of the forbidden mountain. "There are the deer."

"Let's go."

Lenna felt a brief pull of resistance at the idea of venturing onto the forbidden mountain, although she knew there was no need to worry about it. Primitive myths about ancient warriors climbing the mountain and bringing back fire weren't any actual danger to her.

So she followed Desh as he quickly paced toward the foot of the mountain.

They hadn't gone very far up when they walked around a huge cluster of boulders and saw a thickly matted group of trees that had grown up in a very strange position, all curved in the same manner.

"I can't see the deer," Desh said with a sigh. "Maybe we should head back before it gets too late."

Lenna was about to agree when she noticed something that made her jerk to a stop.

Among the thick growth of trees, she saw something emerging that seemed to be made of metal.

Of metal.

She stepped forward and realized she was looking at the barrel of a laser—the large kind that were installed on ships for defense.

Instinctively, she squeezed Desh's upper arm very hard, hardly able to process what she was looking at.

Desh must have seen it too. "Damn," he breathed. "Maybe this is the source of those myths about the forbidden mountain."

Of course it was. All those old stories, passed around among tribes as the young men left to join others, would have a common source. A spaceship must have crashed here a long time ago—much bigger than a pod from a planet dump, big enough to make a lasting impact.

In silent agreement, Desh and Lenna approached, pushing through the trees until they could orient themselves to the position of the ship and then find one of the doors. They had to break off several branches to get in, but they finally were able to hit the emergency release and open the door.

"How old is this thing?" Desh asked, crawling inside.

"Ancient." Lenna coughed at the old, musty smell. They'd entered a small hallway, and she started moving toward where she figured the control room must be. "This looks like pre-Coalition. It must be many hundreds of years old."

"It's big. There must have been dozens of people on board."

"Close to a hundred by the size of it." She was opening latches to see sleeping berths and common spaces that suggested the size of the crew and the passengers on board. "I don't see any bones. They must have survived."

"If it's old enough, maybe the surviving crew and any other passengers is how this planet was originally populated with humans. Do you think it could have been long enough for the memory to turn into myth?"

"Maybe. Maybe they went primitive in order to survive. I'm not sure how long it would take to develop a culture and language like this. Or maybe there were already humans here, and they joined them to survive."

"An anthropologist would have a field day with this planet, if that's the case." Desh was blinking and staring around as they entered what was obviously the bridge. "I don't suppose you can get this thing to fly and get us off this planet, can you?"

Lenna's stomach churned uncomfortably, but she knew the answer without any doubt. She gestured toward a tree that was growing into the bridge. "Even if there was enough power, the hull is breached in too many places. There's absolutely no way."

Desh sighed. "Damn. For a moment, I had a little hope."

She saw the disappointment in his face and wondered why she didn't feel crushed in the same way. Her chest had actually relaxed at the knowledge.

She tried the controls and was surprised when an archaic screen actually powered on. "There's a tiny bit of power left! Can you believe it?"

"Enough to do us any good? Can you contact someone?"

"The comms look totally fried," she said, trying out several instrument panels and attempting to figure out how the very old controls worked. "Assuming I'm reading this in the right way. Oh, but there might be enough power for me to rig some sort of distress signal."

"Sure. Send out a distress call to the Coalition. They'll pick us up and dump us criminals onto another planet." Desh sounded depressed, lower than she'd ever heard him.

The surge of hope and immediate disappointment must have hit him hard.

Much harder than it had hit her.

"I can use a frequency they don't follow." She played around with the instrument panel, connecting a few wires until she'd rigged up a signal she thought would work. "There's an old smugglers' frequency. I'll send out the distress call there. Hall knows it—my old partner. A lot of other smugglers follow it too. Maybe someone will be in the area and stop to look."

"Seriously?"

"It's worth a try." She closed the panel and then turned off all of the systems, except those used for the signal. "I'm not sure how long the power will last, but it will send it out for a while anyway. I wouldn't count on anything, but who knows?"

"We better leave a note or something in case someone comes to the ship looking."

"Good idea."

They searched the common areas until they found an old tablet, on which they composed a brief explanation about who they were, what had happened, and where they could be found.

As she did so, Lenna felt again that clench in her chest.

She thought about Rone, about how he would feel if she were to be suddenly rescued off this planet.

He would never understand.

She pushed the thought away. There was virtually no chance of anyone hearing the signal and responding to it. If Hall was still a smuggler, he might feel enough loyalty to come and help her, but he wasn't a smuggler anymore. He was living on an undeveloped planet now with the love of his life, making wine and generally enjoying himself for the first time.

He wasn't going to still be tuning in to an old smugglers' frequency.

Help wasn't going to be arriving for her and Desh.

She wouldn't have to worry about leaving Rone.

They left the ship and started back toward the cave, walking quickly because it was later than they'd realized. Lenna hoped they'd arrive before dinner time.

Both of them were quiet as they walked, caught up in their own thoughts. And because Lenna was thinking about Rone and how she would feel if she ever got the chance to leave this planet, she wasn't paying attention to what was around her.

Desh was obviously distracted too because neither one of them realized anyone else was approaching.

When two hunters stepped out of the trees near them, Lenna was utterly shocked.

They weren't from their tribe. They looked rougher, meaner, with markings on their skin like that very first Neanderthal who had attacked her after she'd landed.

These were hunters from another tribe.

The Hosh, the Kroo's nearest neighbor and not nice people at all.

They stared at Lenna with a look that terrified her more than anything she'd ever seen.

"We're still in no-man's land," Desh said in a hushed voice, slowly reaching out to take Lenna's arm. "We're going to need to run."

Lenna didn't need to be told this twice. She could see danger in their faces, in their stances. She and Desh started off in a synchronized motion, racing in the direction of the cave.

If they could make it to Kroo territory, they would be safe. No other tribe would cross the boundaries.

In no-man's land, they were vulnerable, but no tribe on this planet would risk war by entering another's territory.

She and Desh were both fast runners, but they were tired from walking all day, and the Hosh hunters were bigger and stronger than them. They caught up in just a couple of minutes.

Lenna squealed as she felt a big hand grabbing her shoulder, pulling her down to the ground.

Desh stopped immediately, turning around with his spear. While Lenna was kicking and scratching at the man who had pulled her down, Desh was advancing on the other one.

Desh might have been a nerd growing up, but he'd learned a lot since living on this planet. He was no weakling, and he wasn't going to let Lenna get hurt.

He didn't have a chance, though.

The man on top of her hit Lenna hard across the face, dazing her, almost knocking her out. Her stomach roiled and tears filled her eyes, but she could see enough to know that the second man was going after Desh too. Even with his spear, Desh couldn't fight off two of them.

Lenna screamed when one of the men managed to get Desh's spear out of his hand and turned it around to stab him with it.

Desh went down in an ungainly sprawl, blood soaking his tunic.

As soon as Desh hit the ground, the first man scooped her up and slung her across his shoulder. Then both of them were walking quickly—away from her cave, away from her tribe, away from safety.

She'd been told more than once that tribes occasionally did this—kidnapped women to refresh their gene pool. Her head pounded, and there was blood on her cheek, and Desh was probably dead.

And as soon as they crossed into Hosh territory, no one would be coming to rescue her.

Not even Rone was going to risk war among the tribes.

Not for her.

The blow to her face had been so strong that she couldn't think clearly, and she definitely couldn't move. She hung over this smelly monster's shoulder, nauseated and disoriented—knowing vaguely that she was being kidnapped, that she was going to be raped over and over again, that she wasn't likely to ever get away.

She could kill herself.

Her mind was so pained and confused and terrified that she actually took comfort in that thought. Maybe she could find a way to kill herself.

She lost track of time and place, but in the back of her mind she was aware of the men occasionally talking. They spoke the same language as her tribe—with a different accent and in a different cadence. She could understand some of what they said.

So she understood when one of them said, "Safe."

They must have entered Hosh territory. Any hope she'd had was now dead.

No one was coming to rescue her.

Survival of the tribe was more important than any one individual, and nothing was worth risking war over.

She had no idea what time it was or where she was, but she was vaguely conscious of being dropped from the man's shoulder onto the ground. She lay on the cold dirt, staring up at this human being who looked more animal than man at the moment.

And then she realized he wasn't going to wait to get her back to the rest of the tribe. He was going to rape her right here.

Despite what felt like a concussion, she wasn't going to let that happen without a fight.

Screaming again, she kicked out at him with both feet as he started to lean over her to grab her thighs.

She hit his groin, and he roared and doubled over. Before the other man could come to help, she scrambled to her feet and started running.

She couldn't see or think or even breathe, but she tried to run in the direction they'd come from. She hadn't made it very far when one of them was knocking her down, hitting her again across the face.

Her whole body went limp in response to the blow. There was nothing she could do after that—except throb with fear and pain.

The man over her was growling viciously. He was angry. He was going to hurt her so badly.

She'd been independent all her life. Self-sufficient. She'd always prided herself on depending on no one except herself. She'd wanted it that way.

But there was absolutely nothing she could do right now to stop this from happening.

The man had grabbed her legs and pulled off her trousers when she found another surge of strength. She started to kick and claw again, even if it meant she'd get hit another time.

It held him off for a minute, since he had to get control of her limbs before he could do anything. She knew it wouldn't hold him off forever.

Then something else happened. Lenna had no idea what it was, but something changed. The man let her go.

She realized why when she was able to open her eyes. There was another man in the clearing, and both of the Hosh had turned on him.

There was noise, motion, intensity shuddering in the air.

Before she could register any specific movements, both of the Hosh had slumped to the ground.

She could smell blood, and it wasn't her own. Both of those horrible men were dead.

And Rone was leaning over her, reaching down to pick her up.

She sobbed into his chest as he wrapped his arms around her, muttering, "Lenna, Lenna, safe" over and over in a hoarse voice.

After a minute, he loosened his arms and looked over his shoulder in the direction the Hosh had been going. "Lenna wait."

She nodded mutely, wiping away the tears and blood on her face as he set her gently on the ground. She found her trousers and pulled them back on.

One by one, he dragged the two dead men away, and she realized after a minute what he was doing. He had to get the bodies back onto no-man's land before any of the other Hosh found them, so there wouldn't be a war.

It was important. The good of his tribe depended on it.

But his tribe wasn't the only thing that was important to Rone.

When he returned, he was using a branch to scrape up the dirt, hiding tracks and blood from anyone who might be investigating.

Then he picked up Lenna in his arms and carried her away.

When they were clear of Hosh territory, had crossed no-man's land, and had entered Kroo territory but hadn't yet reached the cave, he put her down again on a soft pile of leaves. There, he started to sniff and nuzzle at her. He whimpered at the cuts and bruises on her face, making her cry again.

"Lenna hurt," he muttered, "Lenna hurt."

"Desh!" she gasped, trying to straighten up but completely incapable of it. "Desh hurt!"

"Desh no dead. Desh cave. Rone search Lenna. Find Desh. Desh tell. Rone save Lenna." He was still wiping away the mess on her face and sniffing now at her arms and belly.

Lenna exhaled in relief at this news. Rone must have found an injured Desh, gotten the story, and come after her. Desh wouldn't have had time to return to the cave to find Rone, since he'd caught up to her so quickly. Rone had obviously been already looking.

Her head was still spinning and her stomach churning from pain and fright and disorientation.

Rone was now snuffling at her groin. "Hosh hurt Lenna?"

"No," she choked, realizing what had almost happened. "No. Rone save. Glad. *Glad.*" She reached down for his shoulders, and he pulled her into a hug with a groan that was obviously intense relief.

She sobbed some more, and then suddenly it was too much. She jerked away from Rone suddenly and turned behind her to vomit painfully onto the grass.

Rone was making distressed noises as he stroked her hair and back. "Lenna hurt. Lenna hurt."

"Lenna no hurt bad," she finally managed to say. "Cave?"

Rone nodded and stood up, reaching down to swing her back into his arms.

He carried her to the cave and then to his bed. The rest of the tribe gathered round, obviously worried about her. In her half-stupor, she was still glad to see that Desh was on his feet, having been stabbed in the shoulder but not serious enough to be life-threatening. Rone took water and herbs to bathe her injuries, and he took off her clothes to wrap her in blankets from his bed.

He told the others that he'd caught up to the Hosh in no-man's land and managed to rescue her, but Lenna knew the truth.

He'd gone into another tribe's territory.

He'd risked not just his own safety. He'd risk war.

For her.

To rescue *her*.

Because he cared about her that much.

The rest of the tribe went outside to make a fire and prepare dinner. Lenna couldn't eat anything, and Rone wouldn't leave her.

Eventually, he climbed into bed with her, pulling her against him.

When he started to rub his face against her, Lenna managed to say, "No fuck. No fuck."

"Rone no fuck," Rone murmured, still nuzzling her gently. "Lenna sick. No fuck."

She realized he hadn't been trying to initiate sex. He was just covering her with his scent. He was just taking care of her.

"Lenna home," Rone said, over and over again as he held her in his arms. "Lenna home."

She'd been independent all her life. She'd never had to rely on anyone else.

She did now.

But at least she could trust that Rone would always be there for her.

She fell asleep in his arms, safe in that knowledge.

EIGHT

Four days later, Lenna's ribs were still sore and her face was still bruised—but she was feeling content, almost happy, in a way she hadn't been since she'd arrived on the planet.

It felt like something restless had finally been settled inside her. She wasn't sure exactly what it was, but it had happened when Rone had rescued her from the Hosh. After that, her whole world—even this harsh, primitive one—felt better.

At the moment, she was grooming Rone, carefully shaving his jaw. He always sat completely still on the rock near the river they always used, and his dark eyes never left her face as she focused on her task.

When she winced very slightly as she leaned over to reach near his far ear, he murmured, "Lenna hurt?"

"Small hurt," she told him, smiling at his concern. "Lenna good."

"Groom tomorrow?"

"No. Groom now. Small hurt." She finished with the razor edge, wiping the cut bristles away with her thumb

When she lifted her eyes to meet his, she saw that his expression had changed, softened. He raised a hand to her cheek, rubbing her bruises very gently the way she'd rubbed at his bristles.

She smiled and leaned forward to press a soft kiss on his mouth. "Lenna good," she murmured.

He returned the kiss the way he always did—trying to match her motion with a questioning urgency that proved kissing was still new to him. Then he smiled against her lips. "Lenna home."

He'd been saying that a lot, ever since he'd rescued her from the Hosh. She assumed he was still basking in the relief that he had gotten her back.

She understood the feeling.

With one more quick kiss, she smiled back at him and pulled away to pick up the little clay bowl that held the oil. She rubbed him down with it, unsurprised to discover he was already fully erect.

She chuckled as she finished with his legs and leaned back to set down the bowl on the dirt beside her. "Done."

Rone inhaled sharply and narrowed his eyes at her.

She laughed even more at his expression.

He obviously knew she was teasing because there was a warm sparkle in his eyes. But he kept feigning teasing indignation as he said, "Lenna no good."

"Lenna *very* good." Her voice was soft and hoarse as she rose up on her knees and slid her hands beneath his trousers to find his cock.

He gasped again, this time in a different way. His whole body tightened up. "Lenna *very* good."

Freeing his erection, she tilted her head down so she could tease it with her tongue for a minute, enjoying the way his muscles tensed and his breath hitched in his throat. Then she took him into her mouth, sucking around him rhythmically until he could barely control his hips.

He came hard into her mouth, roaring as he climaxed with a complete lack of inhibition she'd never known in a man before Rone.

She loved it. Loved that he took such pleasure in her. Loved that she could make him feel so good.

He was breathing heavily as she straightened up, wiping her mouth as she smiled at his damp, flushed face.

Before she could say anything, he'd pulled her up into his arms, cradling her on his lap in a way that left her feeling so off-balance she could do nothing but cling to him.

He nuzzled her face and neck, sliding a hand down until he'd snuck it into her trousers. He found and rubbed her clit as he kept rubbing his face against hers.

She clutched at him helplessly as the sensations overwhelmed her. She'd already been very turned on from making him come, so it didn't take long until a climax was shuddering through her, making her moan and gasp. He kept rubbing and nuzzling until she'd come again and then again, almost screaming as the last orgasm overtook her without warning.

Finally, she had to reach down to pull his hand away from her groin. She was hot and limp and exhausted and completely sated, still sprawled in his lap, against his chest.

"Rone good," she gasped. "Rone very good."

He chuckled and pressed a little kiss just to the side of her mouth. "Lenna good. Lenna home."

He stroked her hair as she recovered, and it was several minutes before she felt steady enough to pull out of his arms and sit on the rock beside him. She leaned against him as he wrapped an arm around her.

Finally, she said, "Rone?"

"Yes."

"Lenna ask Rone question?"

"Yes. Rone give Lenna world."

She smiled at the words. She'd heard others say the same thing and knew it was mostly just an expression, but it really felt like Rone would give her anything, anything in his world. She was a little nervous about her question, though, so she paused before she said, "Rone help Desh hunt?"

Rone tensed slightly and pulled away so he could look down into her face.

She cleared her throat. "Rone help Desh hunt?"

He shook his head after a moment. "Desh boy. Desh no hunt."

"Desh no boy. Desh man. Desh fight Hosh, help Lenna."

Very slowly, Rone nodded in acknowledgment over the part Desh had played in trying to save Lenna.

"Desh hunt. Rone good hunt. Rone help?"

He was frowning with a familiar look of confusion and jealousy. "Lenna Rone mate."

"Yes, Lenna Rone mate. No Desh mate. Rone help Desh hunt? Desh man?"

Rone rubbed at his face with one hand, clearly torn.

Seeing that he might be caving, she leaned over and kissed his cheek. "Lenna ask good." There was no way to say "please" in their language, so that was the closest she could come.

After a brief hesitation, he laughed softly and shook his head. "Lenna ask good. Rone help Desh hunt."

She made an excited exclamation and wrapped her arms around him in a tight hug, and Rone's reluctance disappeared.

The following afternoon, Rone took Desh out to help him practice hunting. Lenna went with them because it was a lovely, crisp day and she didn't want to stay at the cave and clean turnips.

Rone started by giving Desh tips on how to hold the spear, how to aim it, and how to throw.

Desh was clearly pleased with the assistance, and he listened carefully and tried to follow Rone's instructions.

Lenna watched them at first, but then she got bored, so she picked up Rone's spear and tried to hold, aim, and throw it herself.

As Desh went to pick up his spear after one particularly long throw, Rone glanced back and saw what Lenna was doing.

Making a wordless sound in his throat, he walked over and took the spear from her hand. "Lenna woman," he said with an affectionate smile. "Lenna no hunt."

She wasn't surprised or particularly offended. Rone had spent his entire life believing that this was true. It would never occur to him that anyone would want to challenge this basic truth.

"Lenna woman," she said, reaching to take the spear back. "Lenna try hunt."

"Spear hurt Lenna." His smile had faded into concern. "Men strong. Men hunt."

"Lenna strong." To prove her point, she aimed and threw the spear as hard as she could.

It was a much better throw than she'd managed when she'd practiced with Desh, since the tips Rone had given had helped her with holding the spear in the right way. The spear went almost as far as Desh's had.

Rone's eyes widened in astonishment at the length of her throw.

"Lenna strong," she said again. "Lenna try hunt." Then, realizing his allowing her to do this might cause conflict in the tribe, she added, "No tell Kroo."

Rone thought this through for a minute, and then he nodded. "Lenna hunt. Lenna hunt no alone. Rone help."

"No alone," she agreed, smiling as something fluttered in her chest.

It might just be a small thing, but it felt significant.

People could change. Rone could change. The difference in their worldviews didn't necessary have to be an unmovable obstacle.

He wanted what was best for her, even if it wasn't what he'd always assumed.

She wanted the best for him too.

She reached over to give him a hug without thinking, and he returned it enthusiastically, nuzzling her face fondly.

They were interrupted by a voice from behind them. After a teasing exclamation that sounded like, "Hey!" Desh said, "No mating here. Mate cave. Hunt now."

Both Lenna and Rone laughed and pulled apart, and they continued the lesson in hunting.

For about an hour, Rone showed them how to look for signs of animals nearby, stalk them, move without making noise, and then go in for the kill.

Lenna actually had no desire to kill animals if she didn't have to, but it wouldn't hurt to know how, in case she ever was in the position to need to.

After the lesson was over, Rone sent her and Desh ahead of him to track a small herd of deer in the distance and then try for a successful kill.

Rone was going to wait and come after them in a while so they could try it alone, without his help.

Desh went off immediately, but Lenna paused to look back at Rone.

"Lenna hunt," he said, gesturing toward Desh. "Lenna strong."

Filled with affection more powerful than anything she'd ever felt before in her life, she put down her spear and threw herself in his arms. "Rone good, good, good. Glad Rone mate Lenna."

He chuckled and returned the embrace, being careful with her sore ribs. When he released her, he met her eyes soberly. "Glad Lenna mate Rone. Lenna *home*."

She smiled rather wobbly, strangely emotional. Then she pressed a quick kiss on his mouth and picked back up the spear. "Lenna hunt."

She was happy and excited and fond and off-balanced from feeling things so deeply as she hurried to follow Desh, glancing back once more over her shoulder at Rone—standing alone in the sunshine—before he was out of sight.

When she caught up with Desh, they smiled at each other as they moved in unison to track the herd.

They'd walked about a half-hour when they finally got close.

Lenna suggested a strategy, and she came from one direction to scare the grazers, who immediately ran away from her.

Right toward Desh.

Before she knew what was happening, Desh had thrown his spear right into the throat of a medium-sized female.

Both Lenna and Desh stared down at the dead deer.

"We did it," he murmured, clearly astonished.

"I can't believe it." She didn't look too closely at the dead animal, since it made her remember her poor little fawn too much, and that made her a bit sad. "It was a great throw."

"I couldn't have done it without you."

"Rone will be so proud," she said, smiling and touching his arm in a friendly way.

Before Desh could respond, she heard a rustle from the trees nearby. She whirled around, holding Rone's spear defensively, her heart jumping into her throat at the thought that it might be Hosh hunters again.

The ones who had taken her were dead, but it was possible there could be others.

It wasn't Hosh hunters.

The man who stepped out from the trees was grinning at her in a very familiar way.

"Leave it to Lenna," he said, "to survive a planet dump and then attack her rescuer with a spear like some sort of barbarian maiden."

"I am not a maiden," she said automatically, focusing on the most irrelevant thing first.

"Oh, I believe you," Hall said, stepping closer to her. "So do you want to be rescued or not?"

Hall had been her smuggling partner for a long time before he'd retired. He was still her friend.

"Damn," Desh breathed, coming to stand beside her. "You mean the distress signal actually worked?"

Hall turned his handsome face to the younger man. "Is this a friend of yours?"

"Yes. This is Desh." She was still so shocked she could barely move, barely think. "He got planet dumped here too."

"Great. He can come along if he wants. The more the merrier. But let's get moving, if you don't mind."

"Hallelujah," Desh said, taking the spear out of Lenna's hand and laying it down on the ground. "I'm not going to say no to a miracle. I'm ready when you are."

"I've got a ship nearby. We found the crashed ship and your note, so we were heading toward the cave you described. Just as well you saved us the trip."

"We?" Lenna said, rather hoarsely.

"Me and my buddy Cain. We're in his old clunker, and it doesn't like to be rushed. So the sooner we get out of here the better. It looked like a Coalition fleet was going to pass by this planet in not too long, and I'd rather be gone by the time they get here so they don't think we were up to nefarious doings." Hall always had a teasing, confident manner, but she could see genuine urgency in his eyes.

She couldn't let him and his friend get arrested for coming to save her. She had to do what she was going to do, right now.

She glanced back in the direction where she'd left Rone. "So we… just leave?"

Desh obviously knew what she was thinking about. "I don't think you can tell him you're leaving. He'd never understand. He might actually try to stop you."

"We don't really have time for long goodbyes," Hall said, for the first time looking rather concerned. "If you need to take someone else with us, we need to get them fast."

Lenna was frozen, still looking back in Rone's direction, picturing him standing in the sun, waiting for her.

He would be so confused. So upset. So dismayed.

She would have just disappeared, and he'd have no idea where she was.

"We can't take him with us," Desh said softly, sounding unexpectedly sympathetic. "He'd be miserable on any world but this one."

She knew that was true. She couldn't sentence him to a life he'd hate just so she didn't have to say goodbye to him.

"Lenna?" Hall asked gently. "You do want to come with us, don't you?"

She swallowed hard. "Yes. Yes, of course."

It was all happening too fast. She couldn't think of any other options. Only leaving now—without Rone—or staying on this planet forever.

"Then come with us now—while we can. If you change your mind, you can always come back here."

Hall's words were like a lifeline. The option of maybe coming back if she decided that was what she wanted.

She wouldn't necessarily be abandoning Rone forever.

She didn't belong on this planet. She belonged in the civilized world with Hall and Desh and others like them.

She was a pilot and a smuggler. She belonged on a ship.

She shouldn't have ever had a spear in her hand or a man like Rone in her bed.

It wasn't who she was.

It wasn't who she'd ever be.

"Okay," she gasped, nodding her head. "Let's go."

Both Hall and Desh looked relieved, so that made her think she must have made the right decision.

It didn't take very long for them to reach a small, rather dilapidated spacecraft that Hall's friend Cain evidently used for transporting goods. They buckled in and Cain took off, and soon they were breaking through the planet's atmosphere.

And all the time Lenna was imagining Rone's face.

He would come to find them when they didn't return. He would find the dead deer with Desh's spear still in it. He would find his own spear on the ground nearby.

He might follow their tracks. He was good at that.

But it would only lead to a slightly charred patch of grass where the spaceship had launched from.

He would have no idea what had happened to her.

He would just know she was gone.

NINE

Lenna's stomach roiled sickeningly as they broke through the planet's atmosphere and jumped into hyper-speed.

She wasn't exactly sure how long she'd been on the planet, but it must have been at least four months. That was how long it had been since she'd been in a spaceship, on a mechanized vehicle of any kind. The motion was jarring, disorienting.

Her only comfort was the fact that Desh was leaning back in his seat, eyes closed and wincing visibly so he must be just as affected by the motion and change in atmosphere as she was.

Eventually, she had to lower her head between her legs in an attempt to get her bearings.

"Are you okay?" Hall asked, having turned around to see her position.

"Yeah," she replied breathlessly.

"You're not going to throw up are you?"

"No," she replied with more hope than credibility.

"I never thought I'd see the day when you got sick on a ship." Hall's voice was teasing but gentle.

She lifted her head to glare at him. "I just spent months on a primitive planet, living in a cave and using nothing but stone-age tools to survive. Just how do you think you'd feel if you'd done that?"

"I wouldn't be feeling a thing because I would have rolled over and died a long time ago," Hall said, an appealing smile twitching on the corner of his mouth. "We're headed to the planet where Cain and I live. We've got a day and a half before we reach it, so try to hang on until then."

"I'm hanging on." The spinning in her head had slowed down so she straightened up in her seat again. "So how did you happen to hear the distress call? I thought you were fully retired."

"I am."

"But you're still listening to the smugglers' frequency?"

"Not all the time." Something in his expression looked almost diffident, and it prompted her curiosity.

"So how did you hear it?"

Hall made a face, as if embarrassed by the admission. "I'd heard you were planet dumped a few months ago, so I made a point of checking it out at least once a day, in case you needed my help."

She stared at him, her eyes widening. "Really?"

He frowned. "Of course really. I would have been dead several times over if it weren't for you. Kyla would be dead at least once. Even if I didn't like having you alive in the universe—which I do—I believe in paying off debts." He slanted her a quick look, as if he were checking for her reaction to his words.

It was a sign of how rattled and disoriented she was that her eyes actually teared up at his words.

He evidently saw this. "You haven't turned emotional on me, have you?"

"Of course not." She was relieved when the surge of feeling passed.

"Good. I could always count on you to be efficient and no-nonsense, telling me how stupid I am for falling in love. I never thought I'd see the day when you turned stupid too."

"I'm not stupid," she insisted, forcing down a swell of grief at the thought of Rone still down on the planet, probably searching for her desperately at this very moment.

Her claim prompted a response from Desh, who opened his eyes and arched his brows.

"I'm not stupid," she repeated, trying to convince herself as much as the men.

Hall glanced between her face and Desh's, but all he said was, "Glad to hear it."

When the ship neared a large star, the edges of the gravitational forces caused it to rattle and shake. It was a normal, everyday occurrence in space travel, but it caused Lenna to gasp and put her hand on her stomach.

Hall's teasing expression turned sympathetic. "Damn. You both look like you feel terrible. You'll feel better when we get back on the ground."

"Where are we going anyway?" Desh asked, evidently rousing himself enough to enter the conversation.

"It's an undeveloped planet—no Coalition base, so we're basically left alone."

"Hall and his wife, Kyla, have a vineyard there," Lenna told Desh. "They make wine. The real thing."

"We're just starting out," Hall added. "There's no wine yet. Cain has a ranch there. Real old-fashioned cattle." He nodded toward his big, rough-looking friend, who hadn't said a word more than a grunt the whole time. He was clearly listening to the conversation as he piloted the ship, but he didn't seem inclined to talk if he didn't have to.

Rone would probably like him.

"That sounds like a good place to me," Desh said. "As long as there are working showers and food I don't have to kill or dig up first."

"I think we can offer you that much," Hall replied. "You look pretty young to have been planet dumped. What did you do?"

Desh gave a half-shrug.

"He told me he'd talked back to the wrong person. He was only sixteen at the time."

Hall's eyes widened. "Sixteen? You must have said something pretty bad to someone really important."

Desh turned away with an uncharacteristically evasive expression.

Lenna realized that, after all this time, she still knew very little about this young man. "Who did you insult, Desh?" she asked softly

After a moment, he met her eyes. "The High Director."

Everyone on the ship gasped at this news, even stoic Cain. "The High Director?" Lenna repeated. "Of the Coalition Council? *That* High Director?"

The Coalition was governed by a large council, which was supposed to be made up of representatives from all areas of Coalition space, but had gradually turned into a power-grab from the most ruthless, ambitious people.

The High Director of the council was the most powerful individual in the known universe.

"Yes," Desh admitted, rubbing his hair uncomfortably. "That one."

"What did you say?"

"I... publically humiliated him. And he took it personally because... because he's my father."

At this piece of information, even Cain turned in his seat to stare at the young man.

They were all silent for a full-minute.

Finally, Desh said, "I know. But it's not exactly a family I want to brag about. The Kroo was more of a family to me than he ever was. Needless to say, I'm not planning to head back home for a family reunion."

Hall nodded slowly. "Well, you can stay with us until you get back on your feet. Both of you."

Lenna appreciated the offer, but she couldn't imagine at the moment ever being who she used to be.

For a moment, she wished with an intensity that overwhelmed her that she was still back in the cave.

"The crew?" Hall asked, out of the blue, evidently thinking of what Desh had just said.

"Kroo," Lenna repeated. "It's what the tribe of people we stayed with called themselves. They spoke a different language, so it's not crew like in our…" She trailed off as an idea hit her without warning.

She thought about that ancient ship that had evidently crashed on that planet several centuries ago.

That ship had a crew.

The Kroo.

She gasped, and her eyes flew to meet Desh's. Maybe the word had lasted in their language—transformed by time and context—for that long.

"That would be crazy," Desh murmured, evidently thinking of the same thing. "For them to hold onto that word for so long, even as every other remnant of civilization got burned away."

Cain turned again in his seat to face them and said unexpectedly, "Civilization is only a myth."

Hall, Lenna, and Desh all stared at him in surprise.

Cain shook his head and turned back to the control panel, evidently having said all he wanted to say.

Hall nodded slowly, evidently understanding what his friend was saying. "He's right. He and I saw it first hand in that prison planet. Throw human beings into a situation where they have to fight to survive, and every superficial piece of civilization will eventually get stripped away. That's what you saw on that planet with that tribe, isn't it?"

Lenna thought about the question, confused and guilty and strangely lonely.

Hall and Cain were right. Human beings might always be left with their most fundamental selves if their survival was at stake.

But the Kroo had proved to her that their most fundamental selves weren't all bad, weren't any different from anyone else she'd ever known.

"Maybe," she said slowly, after a long pause. "I guess what's left underneath is what matters, what makes us all human. Some of it's good. Some of it's bad."

Cain looked back from the controls to meet her eyes briefly, and she saw something there like recognition. "Yes," he muttered. "That's right."

∼

It was late the following evening when Lenna finally walked into the comfortable, airy home of Hall and his wife, Kyla. She was so exhausted and out of it that she could barely focus enough to make conversation, so they showed her to her room right away, where she showered and went right to bed.

She slept well because her body urgently needed to rest—not because she was settled or content.

She still felt sick and restless when she woke up the next morning.

She wouldn't have expected to feel that way. She would have thought her time on the planet with the Kroo would have started to feel like a harsh dream. It didn't, though.

This world felt like the dream—the edges all blurred and the colors too muted, nothing bright or solid or real.

She wondered what Rone was doing, if he was okay, and then she cried for a minute, hiding her face in the pillow before she made herself gain her composure and get up.

The synthetic fabric of the clothing Kyla had given her to wear felt strange against her skin—too light, not nearly substantial enough. And she couldn't take more than a sip of the coffee Hall handed her when she made her way to the kitchen.

It was too hot, too bitter. It burned down her throat.

When she put the mug down and asked for water instead, Kyla handed her a glass with a sympathetic smile. Kyla was pretty in an understated way. Quiet. Giving off the sense that her inner life was far richer and deeper than anything she showed on the surface.

She wasn't at all the kind of woman Lenna had imagined Hall might end up with, but the two matched in a very satisfying way. Lenna had always thought so, although she never would have dreamed of telling Hall.

"I can't imagine how hard it must be to get used to modern comforts again," Kyla said, sitting down at the table and gesturing Lenna into the seat beside her. "Hall told me what you've been through. I think it's amazing you did as well as you did."

Lenna smiled—slightly poignant—and met Hall's eyes as he sat across from her. "I've always been a survivor."

"I'm sure it will take some time to get acclimated again," Kyla replied. "But when you do, you'll feel more like your old self."

The words were kind, but Lenna didn't believe them. She wasn't sure she'd ever feel like her old self again.

She wasn't sure she even wanted to.

The idea of getting back in her old ship, taking smuggling jobs, going through life on her own, completely independent, seemed brutally lonely right now.

She missed Rone. She wished he was here right now.

But she never could have taken him with her. It never would have worked.

"Or you could do something else," Kyla added, evidently noticing that Lenna wasn't too excited about her suggestion. "People change. Look at Hall." She gave her husband a teasing, slanting look that made him smile. "You can do anything you want now."

"Yeah," Lenna managed to say, emotion trapped tightly in her throat. "I just can't seem to think clearly right now about anything. My whole mind is a whirl."

"Give it some time," Kyla said. Then she gave Hall another look, this one more like a question.

Hall nodded, as if he'd understood the unspoken words. He leaned forward slightly, reaching his hand out toward Lenna. "I might be able to help calm your mind, if you'd like me to."

Lenna had known Hall for a long time, but ridiculously she'd almost forgotten about his special gift. He'd been born with an extra-sensory ability to feel other people's emotions by physically touching them, but he was more than just a Reader. He could take their feelings, transform them, and send them back.

Hall had never tried to use his gift on Lenna—except for a few times when she'd been injured and had needed immediate relief from the pain so they could escape a dangerous situation.

But Lenna felt so terrible at the moment that she was willing to try anything. She stretched a hand out and offered it to Hall.

Without speaking, he touched the bare skin of her inner wrist very gently with his fingertips.

Lenna gasped as she felt some sort of internal channel open up between them. For a moment, it felt like he was inside her, collecting her incomprehensible tangle of emotions into a ball and then releasing them back to her in an intense wave of relief.

She closed her eyes, feeling better when he withdrew his hand. The relief wouldn't last for long—she knew—but at least it gave her a short respite during which she could think.

Hall's brow was lowered in uncharacteristic seriousness as he met her eyes. "We should have brought him with us," he murmured, slightly hoarse. "We could have tried."

Lenna shook her head, realizing that Hall must have sensed the depth of her feelings for Rone in that brief touch. "No. It wouldn't have been fair to him. He doesn't know of any world except his own. I couldn't just snatch him away, bring him into all this… not just because I… I want him. He would be so… so unhappy. I won't do that to him."

Kyla was frowning now too. "I'm so sorry. I thought they were all kind of brutal and primitive on that planet. I didn't realize you'd found someone special."

"I miss him," Lenna admitted, a tiny part of her mind realizing that she never would have made such a vulnerable admission before she'd been planet dumped. "Actually, I miss all of them. My whole tribe. Even the ones who weren't very nice." She sighed and closed her eyes for a moment, trying to imagine herself back in the cave. "They were primitive—at least in terms of technology—but they were still human. And to tell you the truth, the Coalition might be the most civilized world in human history, but that doesn't stop it from being far more heartless and brutal."

Hall nodded. "I can testify to that."

"Well," Kyla said hesitantly, after a moment of silence, "I know it sounds strange, but you could always go back. If you wanted to, I mean."

Lenna stared at her, trying to process the sudden jump in her chest.

"If you liked it there, if you want to be with your man, with those people, why shouldn't you go back?" Kyla looked over at Hall, as if for affirmation.

"That's always an option," he said slowly.

Lenna gave a huff of bitter amusement. "Right. After you risked your neck coming to rescue me, I'm just going to head right back."

"You could," Hall said. "It would be different, going back there by choice. You'd know for sure it's what you want. It would make the rescue worth it. Plus, we got Desh out of there, and he obviously didn't want to stay."

Desh was still in bed. He'd been on the planet for years longer than Lenna. He had a lot more recovery than her to go through.

Her mind was whirling again, even after being eased by Hall's touch. "I can't," she managed to say. "It would be... people don't do that. They don't go back to world like that—one that's less comfortable, less safe, less..." She trailed off, realizing the safest and happiest she'd ever been in her life was in Rone's bed, in his arms. She took a shaky breath. "People don't do that."

"I was born on one of the most sophisticated, decadent planets in Coalition space," Kyla said softly. "I was a member of a royal family, and I'd never had to work a day in my life. But I left that place, came here to a rustic, undeveloped world where I have to work every day. And it was the best decision I ever made."

Lenna believed her. But this planet was different. It was old-fashioned and undeveloped, but the people who lived here knew about the rest of the world and had access to technology and medicine.

And metal.

And wine.

And showers.

And a claim to real independence.

"I'd have to give everything up," she whispered, mostly to herself, since the others hadn't heard her internal musings.

"It's not about giving up," Hall said, almost as softly as she'd spoken. "It's about choosing what you want. Whenever we make choices, it means there are other things we don't choose. When I chose life here with Kyla, I had to give up my old life. But those things weren't nearly as important to me as what I chose."

Lenna swallowed hard, the words hitting her with a significance that was impossible to ignore.

Maybe it wouldn't be about giving up.

Maybe it would be about choosing.

Maybe that was the life she wanted. Maybe Rone was who she wanted.

More than anything else.

"I don't know," she said at last.

Hall cleared his throat and got up to refill his coffee cup, clearly breaking the intensity of the mood in the kitchen. "Well, think about it. You don't have to decide right away. Just decide what's going to let you go to sleep at night in peace and wake up in the mornings happy to start the new day."

It was a relief, the knowledge that she could think about it. That she didn't have to make life-changing decisions less than an hour after waking up.

Feeling better despite her lingering confusion, she smiled at him. "When did you get so smart anyway?"

Hall laughed and sat down again, his eyes resting briefly on Kyla with affection so strong it was palpable. "It was a long time coming. But maybe I'm getting there at last." His expression changing, he added, "You must have enough savings to buy a small ship, one that could be hidden in those mountains, complete with extra fuel cells. If you decide to go back and something happens to change your situation there, you could always leave again. You wouldn't have to be trapped forever."

Lenna's mouth parted. She'd never even thought about that.

~

That night, Lenna was lying in bed, feeling strange on the soft mattress and uncomfortable in the lightweight covers.

She needed something heavier, courser over her body. She was clean and full and rested, and she felt absolutely miserable.

Even the smell of the room bothered her—the fresh sheets, the flowers near the windows. It all felt sterile, artificial.

She missed the smell of Rone beside her.

She tried to convince herself that something was wrong with her that she missed a big smelly man who was incapable of forming complete sentences—at least the kind of sentences she used to know.

But her attempt failed completely. She just didn't care.

She wanted to go to sleep in peace, and she couldn't do it here.

She tossed and turned most of the night until she finally fell asleep shortly before dawn.

She woke up after sunrise still feeling sick to her stomach, dreading getting up in this world.

She sat up in bed, suddenly knowing for sure what she wanted to do.

Hall was right. She could choose to live a life where she went to sleep in peace and woke up excited about the day. And that life just wasn't here.

She wanted Rone, and the only way she could have him was giving up the life she'd known before.

So she was going to choose *him*.

Three days later, she landed a small spacecraft in the mountains, after scouting out a place to hide it where it wouldn't be likely to be found. It was near the site of that archaic crashed ship, and none of the tribes on his planet dared to come near to that mountain.

She was pretty sure it would be safe.

The ship had taken most of her savings since it had all the newest features—primarily fuel cells that would last longer than her life span. She would have been happy to spend everything she possessed on it, though.

She doubted she was ever going to make the trip off the planet and return to Coalition space. Not while Rone was alive, anyway.

She took the time to pile some big rocks up in front of the one direction the ship could be seen from below, until she was satisfied that it was well hidden.

Then she hurried down the mountain and acclimated herself to directions before she turned back toward the Kroo cave and started to walk.

The air here felt fresher, crisper, realer than it did off-world. The sky was bluer and the grass was greener, and she couldn't help but smile as she saw a small herd of the deer, grazing contentedly nearby.

They felt like old friends—not because she'd personalized any of them but the one baby she'd helped to survive but because they were part of this world. They helped keep the Kroo alive and for that they deserved respect.

Her heart raced excitedly as she picked up her speed.

It was late in the day. Almost dinnertime. Rone was probably with the rest of the tribe, making the fire and cooking their food.

She really hoped he was all right.

She couldn't wait to see him.

He might be angry and upset with her, but she was prepared to deal with that. He was a good man. He would understand.

She was almost to the spot where she and Desh had killed that deer—before Hall had appeared and everything had changed.

She was so focused on getting to the cave that it took her a minute to realize someone had called out to her.

When she recognized the sound, she pulled to a stop, searching the grasslands to her right, from where the voice had come.

Her heart jumped into her throat when she saw Rone running toward her.

He wore his normal animal skins, and he held his spear in his hand. He was racing toward her now, still calling out her name.

She was frozen for a moment, joy and pleasure bursting out so vividly in her heart that she couldn't even breathe. Then she was running toward him too, closing the distance between them.

He scooped her up into his arms when she reached him, making helpless, guttural sounds of feelings so deep no words could embody them. She was almost sobbing as she buried her face in his chest.

And she knew she'd made the right decision.

Even if the rest of the universe might think she was crazy, this was exactly where she wanted to be.

It was several minutes before either of them were composed enough to have a conversation. When they finally pulled apart, Lenna was so breathless she had to sit down on the grass to recover herself.

Rone sat down beside her, reaching over to stroke her hair and peering at her with concern and confusion. "Lenna hurt?"

She hadn't used the primitive language for almost a week, but the sound of it was familiar, comforting, like home. She shook her head. "Lenna no hurt. Lenna good."

"Rone search Lenna. Day and day and day and day. Thought Lenna stolen." His face twisted in obvious emotion. "Thought Lenna dead."

Her throat ached at the knowledge that he'd been out looking for her every day since she'd left, that he hadn't given up, even with no sign or clue about what had happened to her. "Lenna sorry. Lenna no stolen. Lenna no dead."

He was scanning her clothes, which were basic trousers and a top but far different from the animal skin clothes he was used to. His expression changed, sobered slightly, as if he'd had a new thought. "Where Lenna?"

She swallowed hard. "Lenna leave. Lenna come back."

He glanced up at the sky, which was a deeper shade of blue as the sun was getting lower. "Stars?"

"Yes. Stars."

He met her eyes soberly. "Lenna leave Rone?"

She shook her head, making a sobbing sound and reaching out for him. "Lenna no leave Rone. Never. Rone Lenna mate."

This was evidently the right thing to say because Rone made another guttural sound and wrapped his arms around her. He rubbed at her face with his in a familiar way, making her smell like him again, making her his. He murmured as he did so, "Rone Lenna mate. Lenna no leave Rone. No leave Rone."

She wasn't going to leave him. Ever again. She was so happy she was almost crying with it—a fact that was slightly disturbing, since she'd never been that kind of a woman.

Eventually, he pushed her back onto the grass and they lay together in an embrace, nuzzling and murmuring out hoarse reassurances.

She wasn't sure how long they lay there, but the sky was even darker when Rone started to nuzzle lower on her body.

She let him. She wanted him to. She wanted him to touch her everywhere. She wanted to smell like him. She wanted to be his completely.

It wasn't a cold evening, but it was too cool to get naked, but Rone managed to work around that, sliding his hands up beneath her top to stroke her breasts and play with her nipple. Soon, she was really turned on, and they managed to get enough of their clothes off so he could slide his hard cock inside her.

He lay over her in missionary position, and she wrapped her legs around him, and they rocked together, gasping and shaking until both of them came to quick, urgent climaxes.

"Lenna Rone mate," he gasped against her skin, his body softening with his release.

She held on to him tightly. "Rone Lenna mate."

"Lenna home. Lenna home." He raised his head to stare down at her face, as if waiting for her to respond.

She nodded, stroking his head. "Lenna home."

His eyebrows pulled together, and he shook his head. "Lenna *home*."

She thought she understood his words, but she couldn't figure out what he meant. She nodded and repeated again, "Lenna home."

He made a frustrated sound and propped himself up on his forearms. "Rone home Lenna," he said slowly, carefully pronouncing each word. "Rone home Lenna."

She stared up at him in confusion. Direct and indirect objects were always slippery in the language, determined by usage she wasn't always familiar with. So it was often difficult for her to understand some sentences, even if the words themselves she knew.

He grunted again impatiently and lifted a hand to his chest. "Rone… home…. Lenna." On the last word, he moved his hand from his own chest to hers.

She gasped audibly, suddenly realizing something she'd never known before.

Shuddering with emotion, she grabbed his hand and held it to her heart. "Lenna home Rone."

His face broke out into a smile that was breathtaking in its absolute purity. "Lenna home."

"Rone home," she said, her face twisting as she fought another wave of emotion. "Rone home."

With a groan, he pulled her into a tight, desperate hug.

She'd been wrong before. There was a word in their language for love after all.

It was the same word they used for home.

He'd been telling her he loved her all this time.

The rest of the tribe was nearly finished with their meal when Rone and Lenna finally returned.

She was surprised about how happy everyone seemed to be to see her. Even Tamen, who told her he was glad she was safe and back in the cave with them.

They stayed up late around the fire, listening to stories and making music. Then finally everyone went into the cave for bed, and Lenna couldn't remember ever being happier.

Rone rubbed her all over and made love to her again in the dark, and she felt perfectly content, perfectly at peace, as she cuddled up against him under the covers afterwards.

"Lenna home," he murmured, brushing his lips against her hair.

"Rone home." She stroked his jaw. He was starting to get a beard. He was going to need to be groomed tomorrow. "Lenna glad cave," she whispered.

He made an affirmative grunt, still nuzzling her idly. Not foreplay this time, just sweet, drowsy affection.

After a minute, he started to sniff her, but he did this a lot, so she didn't think much of it.

He murmured out, "Baby."

She blinked. She hadn't thought the Kroo used endearments that way her society did. "Lenna no baby."

He lifted his head and took her hand to place it on her belly. "Baby."

She gasped as she realized what he was telling her. "Baby?"

"Baby." It was too dark to see his face but she could tell by the sound of his voice, by the feel of him beside her, that he was smiling. "Baby."

If he was right, she couldn't be very far along, no more than a few weeks. How he could tell, she had no idea, but she somehow knew he wouldn't be mistaken about this.

She'd never wanted a child. Not once in all her life.

And yet her heart skipped several beats in excitement, in joy, as she processed the possibility.

She wanted to have children with Rone, and she didn't want to wait any longer.

"Glad," she breathed, relaxing on the bed again.

"Glad," Rone agreed, stroking her cheek, her belly, her hair.

Eventually, she closed her eyes, realizing there was nothing in her old life that she missed enough to be a problem, nothing that came close to what she had won.

She'd thought the Kroo were like animals when she'd first met them, but she'd been wrong. They weren't any more primitive at heart than Coalition society. They weren't even all that different.

She didn't regret anything.

Everything human that really mattered she had in abundance right here.

EPILOGUE

A wave of deep, radiating pain hit Lenna, momentarily stealing her breath.

She tried to breathe deeply and focus on the broken branch of a low shrub that Rone was showing her.

A couple of times over the last month, she'd felt false labor pains, so when she'd started feeling contractions this afternoon, she hadn't wanted to assume it was the real thing.

But they weren't going away, and she was starting to wonder if their baby was finally coming after all.

"Lenna," Rone said gruffly, still leaning over toward the broken branch. "See? Deer walk here."

She nodded and swallowed hard, experiencing a ridiculous and completely irrational sense of self-consciousness—as if she was reluctant to tell her mate that they were about to have a baby.

"Yes. Deer walk," she said breathlessly, when the contraction passed.

She was far too pregnant to practice hunting in her condition, but Rone had taken her out a few times to teach her how to track. They were some of her favorite afternoons, and she hadn't wanted to miss out on one today, even though she felt bloated and heavy and sore all over.

Rone straightened up, frowning at her. "Lenna… bored?" He spoke the last word carefully, since it was unfamiliar to him.

As he'd been teaching her how to hunt and track, she'd been teaching him words from her own language—words that embodied complex or abstract thoughts that didn't have words in the Kroo's language.

It was far more challenging than she would have expected to teach him what freedom and peace and condescension and boredom meant. It felt important to her, though—like she could influence him as much as he'd influenced her, like they could genuinely share a life and relationship.

She smiled. "Lenna no bored."

His brows lowered even more. "Lenna... exhausted?"

Chuckling, she shook her head. "Lenna no exhausted." Then she winced when she thought another contraction was starting, relieved when it wasn't quite yet.

He'd evidently seen her slight wince. "Baby here?"

"Yes." She reached out to touch his arm. "Baby here. Cave."

He nodded soberly and took her arm, turning them in the direction of the cave and starting to walk. They weren't more than a couple of miles away, but she started to feel shaky when another contraction tightened painfully.

She should have said something before. She shouldn't have delayed. She was going to have this baby one way or the other, and better it happen at the cave than right here on the grass.

The truth was she was terrified.

So many babies didn't make it past the first week here on this planet.

She already felt deeply connected to hers and Rone's. She would be devastated if she lost their child.

They had to walk slowly because she had to stop every time a contraction hit. The pain was eventually too much to walk through. At first, the walking had seemed to help distract from the pain, but now it was too intense for that to work.

She clung to Rone's arm and gasped and shook, wishing for the first time since she'd returned to this planet that she was in a hospital, that she had medication, that she had at least a few of the comforts of the civilized world.

Most of the time, she didn't even miss them anymore, but this was terrible.

Rone made helpless sounds in his throat every time she suffered through a contraction. He stroked her hair and her back, and she could tell he felt horrible because there wasn't anything he could do to help.

They were about a mile away from the cave still, and the contractions were coming more frequently, when he made a sudden grunt and released his hold on her to lean over and pick something out of some undergrowth.

He looked encouraged when he brought her over a couple of leaves.

She was damp and trembling, having just gone through a contraction, and she just stared at the leaves in confusion.

"Chew," he said, thrusting them out to her. "Help hurt. Chew."

She took the leaves immediately, realizing he knew far more about medicinal herbs on this planet than she did. She took one leaf and chewed on it, making a face at the bitter taste.

"No eat," Rone said softly. "Chew."

Understanding that she wasn't to swallow, she chewed a little more vigorously, amazed when after a minute she felt a mild wave of relief. It didn't take the pain away but it did soften the edges, making her feel a bit fuzzy but not quite so overwhelmed.

With the help of the leaves, she and Rone made it back to the cave. Mara had been outside, peeling vegetables for the stew tonight, but she stood up immediately when she saw Lenna and Rone approaching.

She ran over, her eyes taking in Lenna's pale, perspiring face and Rone's supportive arm around her. "Baby here?"

"Baby here," Lenna gasped.

Mara made a few tsking sounds and took Lenna's arm, leading her into the cave. Rone followed without a word.

Two contractions hit Lenna on the short walk into the cave, a sign which evidently gave Mara all she needed to know about when the baby was coming.

She shooed away a couple of younger women who'd been working in the cave, and then Mara turned to Rone. "Rone leave."

Rone frowned, looking in concern between Lenna and Mara. "Rone stay."

Mara shook her head. "Rone man. Baby woman job. Rone leave."

Lenna was dealing with another contraction so she couldn't, at the moment, contribute to the conversation. Instead, she reached out to take Rone's hand.

Rone made a grunt as he squeezed hers tightly. "No. Rone stay. Support Lenna."

He gave her a quick look, as if affirming that he'd used the word correctly.

He'd used it exactly right. When her breath returned, Lenna gave him a wobbly smile. "Rone stay," she said. "Lenna need Mara and Rone."

This evidently was enough of an explanation to cause Mara to give up the argument. She looked a little rattled at Rone's presence in a situation that men in this tribe weren't supposed to be involved in, but she led Lenna over to an area in the back of the cave where there weren't any beds.

Since Lenna had been part of the tribe, two women had given birth. The first had been the stillborn baby, and the second had been healthy. She basically knew the procedure here, so she didn't question or complain as Mara helped her into the birthing position—which was a very undignified squat.

She'd walked for so long that there wasn't any extra time. She almost immediately felt the intense desire to push, and so that was what she did.

It hurt horribly, but Lenna was in a strange intense daze where she couldn't really process specific sensations or actions. It didn't take very much time at all before the baby was crowning—and then was far enough out for Mara to pull out all the way.

The baby was a girl.

The baby was healthy—she knew this from the smiles on Mara's and Rone's faces as they cleaned her up before handing her to Lenna.

The baby was hers. Hers and Rone's. She really had no idea how it had happened.

She'd fallen to this planet less than sixteen months ago, completely independent, completely alone in the world.

And now she had a family.

Two weeks later, she was propped up in their bed, nursing her baby.

The infant was pink and loud and bigger than Lenna had expected. She'd been born healthy, and she'd taken to nursing really well. There was no reason to assume she wouldn't survive.

Lenna loved her daughter more than she'd ever known was possible.

She and Rone would have to figure out a name soon. The Kroo waited two weeks before they named their children, and by now Lenna understood why. After two weeks, you could be at least reasonably confident that the baby had a decent chance of surviving.

Her daughter had made it that far. She and Rone could name her.

She was a greedy little thing, her tiny mouth suckling eagerly and occasionally dribbling milk down her chin.

She must take after Rone.

Out of the blue, Lenna wondered how Hall and Kyla were doing, whether they would ever have a baby. She couldn't really picture Hall as a father, but no one would ever have imagined Lenna having a baby either.

People could change.

Then she wondered how Desh was doing. She missed him often. The tribe wasn't quite the same place without him.

When she'd left, he hadn't yet known what he was going to do. She wondered if he would go back to school, be the academic he'd been before.

Life had changed him too—and hopefully it was for the better.

On that thought, Lenna looked up and saw Rone coming into the cave, making his way to the bed. It was dinner time, but Lenna had left early to nurse the baby in peace.

The Kroo didn't care about privacy—for anything—but it was easier nursing when she didn't have dozens of interested eyes on her.

Healthy babies were rare enough that everyone was still fascinated.

Rone was smiling as he lowered himself to sit beside her. "Baby good?"

"Baby good," she replied, using her free hand to stroke the soft forehead. Feeling unusually soft, she leaned toward Rone, pleased when he wrapped his arm around her.

"Baby hungry," Rone said, a faint trace of awe in his tone as he watched their daughter nurse.

Lenna laughed. "Yes." She tilted her head down and adjusted her arm so she could press a little kiss on the infant's head. "Hungry like Rone."

Rone made a huff that could have been teasing indignation.

She leaned over and pressed a kiss on his jaw.

He held his face in place so she would kiss it again.

Relaxing against him, she changed positions so the baby could suckle from her other breast.

They were silent for a few minutes, except for a few gurgles and slurps from their daughter.

After a while, Lenna finally put into words a question she'd been wondering for the last two weeks. "Rone glad baby girl?"

The question evidently surprised Rone. He turned his head toward her with a jerk.

"Rone glad baby *girl*?" she asked again, placing more emphasis on the last word to make sure he understood what he was asking.

She really didn't know what he would feel. This was still a male-dominated society—even though Rone himself had changed in ways she never would have imagined when she'd first met him.

Rone turned his eyes back to their daughter. "Yes," he murmured. "Rone glad."

"Lenna glad." She stroked the tiny head with her fingertips again. If their baby had been a boy, he would have left their tribe when he hit puberty. As much as Lenna tried to really feel part of the Kroo, she would have hated that.

"Girl stay," Rone said, as if he'd read her mind. "No leave. Rone glad. Baby *home*."

Lenna couldn't have said it better herself.

ABOUT THE AUTHOR

Claire has been writing romance novels since she was twelve years old. She writes contemporary romance and women's fiction with hot sex and real emotion.

She also writes romance novels under the penname Noelle Adams (noelle-adams.com). If you would like to contact Claire, please check out her website (clairekent.com) or email her at clairekent.writer@yahoo.com.

Books by Claire Kent

Revenge Saga
- Sweet the Sin
- Darker the Release

Escorted Series
- Escorted
- Breaking

Nameless Series
- Nameless
- Christening
- Incarnate

Hold Series
- Hold
- Release

Fall

Standalones
- Seven
- No Regrets
- Finished
- Complicated
- Taking it Off

Printed in Great Britain
by Amazon